AUTHORS' NOTE

Step into our web of lies, betrayal and murder.
One tale twists into another in this macabre collection of
horror so each story must be
read in order.

DIE, MY LOVE

ZOE BLAKE   ADDISON CAIN   CELIA AARON
SJ COLE   JULIA SYKES   JANE HENRY
ASHLEIGH GIANNOCCARO

THE PERFECT WIFE

BY ZOE BLAKE

I will tell you a secret if you promise not to tell Dr. Chaucer.

I'm not mad.

I'm smart.

I know the voices are liars.

It's just that I get confused sometimes, that is all.

Just confused.

But I am very smart.

Each morning I remind myself my name is Julia Boyd. I live at 5436 N. Cherrywood Lane. At least I used to live there. I'm not sure anymore. Sometimes I think I am in my bed but then it doesn't feel the same. The blankets are thinner and the bed frame creaks. I don't remember my bed creaking before. But the nurses keep telling me I'm home, so maybe this is Cherrywood Lane? I also know that I'm thirty-four and have blue eyes.

Would a mad person know all that?

I know I wouldn't get so confused if only *he* would leave me alone. He's always watching me. Even in the darkness I can see his small beady red eyes.

Watching.

Listening.

Judging.

I can hear him in the hallway, whispering to the nurses, telling them what I did.

What he made me do!

He's a liar, just like the voices. I scream at him all the time. I want him to show his face, so I can scratch his eyes out. Do you think he knows I want to do that? To scratch his eyes out? Do you think that is why he never appears? Always just out of reach - in the shadows.

Laughing and taunting me.

I'm not mad.

I'm smart.

Only a smart person would know when someone they can't see is watching them.

I just get confused sometimes…

It helps if I pace around the room. It's a very small room. I thought I used to have wallpaper in my bedroom. Pretty paper with colorful birds and glossy green leaves. Now the walls are a bright white. They hurt my eyes. *He* must have ripped the wallpaper down. He doesn't want me to have pretty things. He never wanted me to have pretty things. If he appeared right now, I would scratch his eyes out.

It's cold and quiet in here. I can only hear muffled voices on the other side of my door. Probably gossiping about me… about what I did.

What he made me do!

Sometimes I like to pretend it is the tv on in the next room. I like to pretend that everything was the way it was before… before that night.

The crippling silence is broken by a harsh rap on the door. A woman I don't recognize enters. They never wait for me to call out enter and they never listen when I say go away.

"Good morning, Julia. How are you feeling today?"

Her voice is soft and light. It grates on my nerves. It sounds bright, like how the walls would sound if they could talk.

I turn my back on her and face the corner, tracing the mortar between the cinderblocks. It should feel rough, but thick coats of paint have made the tracks smooth with just a few tiny bumps. I miss my paper birds.

"Julia, I know you hear me. Turn around and take your medicine."

I ignore her.

"Julia."

Her voice has lost its tinkling quality. Her true nature is peeking through the facade. Faker.

Glancing at her over my shoulder, I see she is wearing a pale pink sweater with a large heart pin on the collar over her nurse scrubs.

"You shouldn't wear pastels. They make you look sallow." I hardly recognize my own voice as I speak. It sounds dry and rough from disuse.

Seeming to brush off my advice, she says, "Now, Julia, you know today is Valentine's Day. I can brush your hair and make you look pretty if you like. I'm sure you will have a special visitor later."

Instinctively, my hand went to the back of my neck, to feel for the ponytail that is no longer there. They cut off all my hair when I came here. *He* told them to do it. I'm sure of it.

Wrapping my arms around my waist, I shake my head no, not wanting to hear again the scratchy squeak my voice has become.

"Alright then. Take your medicine, and I will leave you alone."

I ignore her.

"Julia. Don't make me tell Dr. Chaucer you are being troublesome again," she warned.

Spinning on my heel, I snatch the small paper cup from her hand, sparing only a glance for the sickly green little pill before swallowing it. Crumpling the cup and tossing it back at her, I stomp back to my corner, hating the slippers on my feet. I miss the sounds my high heels would make on a hard floor. The loud click-clack as each foot struck the tiles with purpose. You didn't have to speak when you wore heels. People would know if you were preoccupied or mad or in a hurry just by the sound of the click-clack. Click-clack.

The sallow-faced nurse leaves without another word.

The next time the door opens, the person doesn't even bother to knock.

It's Dr. Chaucer.

He thinks I'm mad, but I'm not… I'm smart.

"Patient 463. Julia Boyd. Admitted December 24, 2018, by her husband, Jack Boyd. Displaying symptoms of psychosis with command hallucinations brought on by extreme stress. She had exhibited no violent outbursts towards herself or others at the time of admission. We have her on a 12.5 mg dose of clozapine twice a day." Dr. Chaucer drones on as he reads from a small clipboard. He is encircled by three tired looking residents. With hunched shoulders and glazed eyes, they only show signs of life when Dr. Chaucer glances up at them. Fakers.

Taking off his glasses, Dr. Chaucer tucks them into his white lab coat pocket before asking, "So, Julia. Are you being a good girl today?"

Except it's not Dr. Chaucer. It's *him*. Jack. Smirking at me. He has finally come out of the shadows.

I lunge for him, my fingers curled into claws.

As I keep telling you, I'm not mad.

Only smart people recognize when one person is masquerading as another.

Besides, it's not my fault.

He made me do it!

* * *

"You really outdid yourself with dinner tonight, baby."

Jack slides back from the dinner table with a groan, rubbing his stomach as if he had a beer belly. He doesn't of course. He's fit and trim and very handsome. It's not why I married him, but it doesn't hurt.

Laughing as I carry the heavy pewter platter with the remnants of our roasted turkey back into the kitchen, I toss out to him over my shoulder, "Glad you liked it. Now you can help clean up."

Coming up behind me, he wraps his arms around my waist as he nudges aside my long ponytail to kiss the soft skin behind my ear. I love when he does that.

"The dishes can wait. Let's go into the living room and enjoy the tree. If you are a good girl, I'll let you open another present early," he said, his voice warm with teasing affection.

"But the dishes," I complain half-heartedly. It is our first Christmas together, and I wanted it to be special. I bought every Martha Stewart holiday cookbook I could find. Everything had to be perfect. The turkey. The mashed potatoes. Even the chocolate chip cookies. It had to be perfect. Otherwise everything would be ruined. The voices would sneer that I had failed again. Telling me I didn't deserve Jack.

I join him in the living room with two glasses of egg nog. I made it myself, right down to the whipped cream topping.

Everything has to be perfect.

Jack patted his lap and I obey, perching prettily on the edge of his knee.

For a moment, all was quiet and still. I stare at the glinting lights of the tree. I had decorated it in silver and white with hints of gold. I am especially proud of these crystal icicles I found in a tiny antique shop downtown. The sharp, clear crystal reflected the lights and made the whole tree seem to shimmer and dance.

It was perfect.

Out of the corner of my eye, I watch as Jack took a sip of the egg nog I had prepared. Holding my breath, I wait.

He doesn't say anything.

Rising, I cross to the tree to adjust the ribbon on one of the silver glitter bows.

Nervously, I wait as he takes another sip.

Still, he says nothing.

Trying to keep my voice from sounding shrill, I casually ask, "Do you like the egg nog, dear?"

There is a long pause. "It's fine, baby."

The tips of my fingers reach toward one of the icicles. The pine branch trembles, making a small silver bell ornament sound off in the silence.

Biting my lip, the coppery taste of blood mixes with the sickeningly sweet cream of the nog. My stomach pitches. "Just fine?" I ask.

"It's fine, baby. I would have used rum to spike it, but whiskey is good too."

So, it wasn't perfect.

Jack picks up the new hunting knife I had just given him, testing the sharp edge and admiring the heavy weight of the animal horn handle. The disgusting egg nog I had ruined sits beside him. Ignored.

I turn back to the tree. Now I could see the dark spaces where I hadn't arranged the lights just right. The areas where there was too much silver and not enough gold accents. The crooked, amateur bows. I run a single fingertip down the cool surface of the icicle. Only this was perfect.

Clear, smooth and bright.

I pull the ornament off the tree and test the weight in my hand, pressing the pad of my thumb against the sharp point. Watching as my thumb turns purple as it fills with blood and gently swells around the tip.

"Hey, baby, did you want to watch a Christmas movie?" I love the sound of his voice. It was always dark and low, like he was whispering a secret just for me. I especially love when he calls me baby. I was his. His baby.

His perfect wife.

Smiling sweetly, I cross over to him. In the soft candlelight, his eyes are a warm whiskey brown. They were one of the first features I noticed about him.

Whiskey brown.

Whiskey.

Like the whiskey in the egg nog.

The egg nog I fucked up.

Ruining our perfect first Christmas.

Raising my arm, I plunge the crystal icicle into Jack's right eye. His beautiful whiskey brown eye. My arm shakes with the effort as I push it in deep despite his screams and struggles.

I don't even lose my grip when the warm blood begins to pour over my hand.

I did it perfectly.

* * *

"Take this patient to room 200. I want her in five-point restraints immediately," yells Dr. Chaucer as the sallow-faced nurse ruthlessly grips me by my upper arm. Kicking and thrashing, I fight with all my might. How dare they lay hands on me in my own bedroom?

"Leave my house immediately! I'm going to tell my husband!" I rave.

I claw at the walls as they try to lift me, confused as to why I was feeling hard stone and not the rippled texture of wallpaper.

I was being dragged over the threshold. Startled, I forget to struggle. My hallway had a thick taupe carpet with framed pictures of our honeymoon in Ireland, not piss-colored walls and dirty linoleum floors.

Something isn't right. This isn't my home.

I'm not mad.

I'm smart.

I'm just a little confused.

All around me I hear aggressive shouts.

"Secure her arms."

"Careful, she bites."

"Julia, stop kicking."

"Get the needle."

"Jesus Christ, the bitch bit me."

Desperately, I search around me. "Jack!" I scream. "Jack! Help me!" I know he will come when I call. He loves me. I'm his baby. He said so. The perfect woman for him.

The perfect wife.

"Jack!" There is a sharp pain in my throat as my untried voice struggles to achieve a pitch above the shouts and orders about me. Once again, I reach blindly for the walls, trying to latch on to something, anything.

Torn paper and lace hearts litter the floor as I rip down the Valentine's Day decorations around the nurses' station.

Fingers dig into my flesh as I am forced to lie on my back. The bare rubber mattress is frigid, the cold cutting through my thin hospital gown. I kick out. Feeling the delicate bones of a nurse's nose snap beneath my heel. Crimson blood pours from the orifice, soaking into my terry cloth slippers.

"Fucking crazy bitch," shouts the nurse as she grips her nose and backs out of the room. The remaining nurses tighten the straps around my middle and wrists. With a sneer, the sallow-faced one forces my legs open, thick canvas straps are wrapped around each ankle before being pulled tight and secured.

Then I am alone.

I twist my wrists, testing the restraints. It's hard to breathe with the band across my chest, holding me down.

"Jack," I whisper into the silence. I can see his beady red eyes staring at me from high in the corner by the ceiling.

He's watching me.

Why won't he help?

I can hear the door open but cannot lift my body to see who has entered.

"Someone has been a very bad girl today."

It is Dr. Chaucer.

"Have you forgotten the lesson I taught you just last week?"

I refuse to answer.

"Let's see if I can remind you. First let's turn off these cameras."

He reaches into his coat pocket and pulls out a small remote.

Jack's eyes disappear.

He has abandoned me.

I turn my head away.

Dr. Chaucer cannot fool me.

I'm smart, not mad like his other patients.

A strong hand grips my jaw and forces me to turn my head back. The moment I see what is in his hand, I start to whimper. Memories flood my head, but I'm confused. These can't be my memories. This didn't happen to me. It didn't. I don't know this man.

"Open your mouth."

I shake my head no.

His fingers press against my cheeks. The soft flesh inside splitting on the edges of my teeth.

My mouth is forced open.

I can hear the sickening clatter of metal against bone as he pushes a ring gag between my teeth. The tang from the metal invades my mouth. Leather cuts into the sides of my lips, tearing them as he secures the buckle behind my head. I try to speak... to scream... to plead... but it all comes out as a non-sensical gurgle.

I watch as he undoes his tie. Leaning over my prone body, he wraps the silk around my throat. The silk feels cool at first.

Then he tightens the slip knot. It pulls at the skin around my throat as it presses against my windpipe.

"This is just in case my bad little girl needs some encouragement," he jeers as he reaches for the zipper of his pants.

I see the bulbous engorged head first. It's purple with a moist tip. My body tries to recoil in horror, but the restraints and his grip on the silk tie around my throat prevent any movement.

Memories cross my vision. Flashes of pain. Of humiliation.

No. This isn't happening.

I'm just confused.

This isn't happening.

His disgusting cock is forced between my lips. I cringe at the musky taste as his flesh is pushed deeper into my mouth. My shoulders hunch forward as I dry heave, choking on his shaft.

"That's it. Swallow it," growled Dr. Chaucer.

The wide head pushes against the sensitive back of my throat, cutting off my air. I fight against the restraints as my body struggles for breath. The short inhales through my nose are insufficient. My lips stretch and split around the gag as he ruthlessly thrusts his hips forward. His zipper bites into the skin beneath my jaw as he pushes in deep. I can taste blood from the cuts on the underside of my tongue as it scrapes along the sharp edge of my own teeth.

Dr. Chaucer grunts as he twists his fist into the fabric of his tie, tightening his grip on my throat.

My eyes roll back as air is pushed from my lungs and replaced only with my silent screams. I choke as his cum coats my tongue and the back of my throat. My empty stomach heaves.

The moment he pulls free, the final reserves of oxygen leave my body in a sputter. His cum spews from my mouth to slide down my cheek.

I can feel it cool on my skin as he rights his pants.

"Next time you misbehave on my ward, I'll fuck your ass raw," warns Dr. Chaucer as he leaves the room, slamming and locking the door behind him.

His dried cum on my cheek begins to itch.

* * *

I am no longer the perfect wife.

The voices are shrill inside my head.

No longer perfect.

No longer perfect.

Better off dead.

I'm no longer confused. I know what I have to do.

I grip the top of the screw with my fingernail. The metal edge presses into the pads of my fingertips as I slowly loosen it. It makes a high-pitched squeak as it spins in its tight hole beneath the bed frame. I stop and listen. No nurses come. I continue to slowly loosen it. Eventually it drops into my palm.

It's long, black and rough. I press the pad of my thumb against the sharp point.

The crystal icicle ornament was pretty, smooth and clean. Perfect.

I don't deserve perfect anymore.

I deserve black and rusted.

Flipping my left arm over, I stroke the thin blue vein which runs along my pale wrist with the tip of the screw. It leaves a tiny white scratch behind.

I make another scratch. Then another. And another. Each deeper than the last. Blood tickles my arm as it begins to bead along my skin as I spell out the name "Jack".

I press the tip against the pulse in my wrist. The skin swells around it. I push harder. Harder. The edge of the screw bites into the pads of my fingers. Still I press harder. The tip breaks the surface. Blood pools then drips onto my lap.

I don't even feel it.

I feel nothing.

I push the screw in deeper. Wondering absently if it is long enough to come out the other side of my wrist. Gripping the slippery top, I yank it out. My flesh tears. Bright crimson blood bubbles forth.

My left hand is going numb. I can't grip the screw as easily. I push in the tip then press with my palm till I feel the skin give way. Slick with blood, the screw slides in more easily. I rest my head against the cinderblocks. As my eyes begin to close, I see the walls transform.

Bright beautiful tropical birds start to dance and sing as they hop from one branch to another. Large glossy green leaves capture the sunlight. I can almost feel the warmth on my cheek.

My death will be perfect.

* * *

No. No. There is too much noise.

Stop. I just want to sleep.

I'm tired of being confused.

I'm tired of the voices yelling at me.

"Jesus fucking Christ. Baby! Baby! Don't do this. Get the fucking doctor. Baby! Open your eyes, baby. It's Jack, your husband. Open your eyes for me."

He slips in my blood as he falls to his knees and gathers me close. It feels like I'm underwater. I can hear him calling to me from a distance. His face is blurry and indistinct.

My head lolls to the side.

The ugly linoleum floor is covered in splashes of color. I try to focus through the haze. The colors swirl and contract. The colors are roses. Next to them is a large heart-shaped box of candy.

I smile as the life inside my body drains onto the flower strewn floor.

My perfect husband has brought his perfect wife the perfect Valentine's Day gift.

I knew the voices had lied.

I just wish I hadn't listened.

ABOUT ZOE BLAKE

**USA Today Bestselling Author
& Amazon Top 100 Author**

There is something delicious in our desire for the corrupt, our ravenous appetite for the brutal, the profane, the unspeakable. The taboo. I write the type of books that give you a frisson of unease; that will have you questioning your own resolve as I take you on a dark ride of twists, kinks and perversions of both the flesh and mind. Enjoy the blush and tremble as you read each decadent word. XOXO Zoe

Join Zoe's Facebook Reader Group for weekly signed paperback giveaways.

Join her newsletter for free dark romance books and release updates.

THE CONNOISSEUR

BY ADDISON CAIN

She is perfect. A vision.

I knew she'd choose that dress for tonight. A floaty ivory thing—not too high on the thigh or too low in the bust. Demure, but overly suggestive in that it shouted virgin, damsel, *make me your whore*.

Nervous as she was, *and she should be nervous*, her bodice strained with each deep breath. The gossamer fabric had no give, and she was generously endowed. Under the right circumstances it would likely tear like tissue paper. Part of the appeal, I suppose.

Already my fingers itched, and soon enough I'd rend it to bits.

And what would I find underneath?

Full breasts caught up in some kind of lace brassiere.

I could see the scalloped edges press through the fabric

each time she took another of those tremendous deep breaths. My angel.

And yes, she was mine. Had been for over a year.

Yet she had worn that dress for *him*.

He even had the nerve to smile at her as he arrived ten minutes late, pulling out the seat across from the flustered brunette and plopping down like a plebe. More pointedly, she had the nerve to smile back as if his terrible manners were charming.

And it was a gloriously honest smile. One full of relief. One highlighted by flushed cheeks and shining eyes.

I did so love to see her smile.

Honestly, I searched for that expression often. Not the practiced pleasantries that normally passed between us, but the genuine curve of her normally unpainted lips. My angel had a pleasant countenance, symmetrical, wholesome. Our genetics would combine to make truly attractive children.

My light hair, her golden eyes. British and Nordic, a dash of Hispanic from her grandmother. Obligatory offspring would enjoy my brilliance and her enduring sweetness. The best schools waiting in store for them, and at least one would graduate summa cum laude from Harvard Medical School just as I had. It might take four children to rear the perfect one, but she was young, and we had plenty of time to procreate.

A twitch in my briefs led me to subtly shift on the cushioned dining chair, my growing erection hidden by the white cloth napkin folded exactly in half and placed across my lap.

Tailored suit, crisp, white dress shirt impeccably starched, I wore my finest Turnbull and Asser tie. It matched the honeyed shade of her eyes, chosen especially for this evening.

How had she prepared?

What color were her panties under that dress?

Not harlot red. Not on my angel.

Pink perhaps, or a smooth ivory the same shade as her filmy dress.

Had she bought it new for tonight? For him?

For *me*, more like. That dress would be mine; that smile. Her sultry voice that was almost too rich to be considered decent.

The creamy slit between her thighs…

Candlelight flickered, the soft notes of the live piano gentling the air.

She laughed.

Dared laugh at something the boy had said…

I knew his name: Buck Cummings. You heard that right. Buck. Cummings.

Vulgar, just like his overloud guffaws in this five-star restaurant he'd booked for their date.

Blond hair like mine, a decent jaw. But he lacked my refinement. Certainly lacked education and style. His sport coat screamed used car salesman, bulging where it was too tight on his arms, and hanging loosely where it did not fit his waist. Some women might find the ape former high school athlete turned security guard handsome. By the way my angel flushed at his praise of her becomingly styled hair, she did.

Fortunately for her, I had never been lacking in that regard. No paunch like most men past the age of thirty possessed. Trim and trained. I looked as good under my suit as any man might. She would appreciate that when I held her down and worked my way inside.

Watching him from where I sat, I imagined he was doused in drugstore body spray, felt it tickle my nostrils even from this distance. And felt pity for my angel to have to sit there and tolerate such a cretin. But she had a lesson to learn.

One she would learn over candlelight and cheap wine. The bottle their waitress had just delivered was the least expensive offering on a rather impressive menu—and considering her knowledge on the subject, how she must internally cringe. She would learn her lesson over poorly chosen hors d'oeuvres. Learn it when she was expected to order her own food.

What had become of men to even allow their female companions to glance at the menu? The man should order. Always.

Reading the boy's lips, I shook my head in distaste. Everything he had requested was wrong. No, the best dining experience on this fine menu was clearly the first course of escargots, followed by an heirloom tomato and burrata salad. For her, the seared sea scallops would follow, while I dined upon steak au poivre. Only a Neanderthal would order tenderloin as *he* had. And she, she had been far too generous, ordering a thrifty pasta dish. The swine had not even thought to order sides. The waiter had needed to gently suggest he do so.

Disgusting.

My own jacketed server came to interrupt my musings and block the view. "Would you care for more wine, sir?"

"Yes"—I leaned back to see past the grinning mustachioed man—"thank you."

A Gabriel Rausse Cab Franc out of Virginia. Irregular, I know, but my angel had suggested it the first time I'd patronized her place of employment. That rainy day, she had whispered to me as if sharing a secret that this particular vintage was her favorite. Tonight, I drank it in her honor, sorely tempted to send her a glass so she might be saved from the swill *he'd* ordered.

But punishment first, then breaking. Followed by a strict regimen to cleanse her mind of anything outside my sphere. Once that was through, my sweet girl would be spoiled befitting her station as wife of Our Lady of Perpetual Sorrow's medical director.

The ring had weighed down my pocket for weeks.

A sapphire worthy of a princess. Not a commonplace diamond, not for her. Diamonds littered the beaches of Africa, common through and through. The ring that would grace her finger is unique, like her stunning aquiline nose.

The bow of her lips.

The way she smelled when I covertly leaned over the counter of her wine shop to bask in that glory.

She was good enough to eat.

And sweet.

More importantly, she was smart—yet not over-educated for a woman. High school diploma, a few courses at the local community college. We'd share splendid conversation over lovely dinners she'd prepare.

Across the five-star restaurant, their first course was delivered. While she poked at mussels in the typical white wine butter sauce, I enjoyed a warm crab soup. How I pitied her, watching her fingers grow slippery fighting the shells.

That dish had a time and place. Even I enjoyed such steamed shellfish with a beer while watching the game. But never, *never*, in a restaurant of this caliber. She would be flicked with sauce when the shells came apart. It would mar her tissue paper dress.

That barbarian boy was eating them with his fingers and no doubt dripping on his tie!

Disgusting…

When she was properly trained, obedient, and docile, I would reward her by seating her at that very table they shared in her shame this night. Dazzlingly her with the manners of a true gentleman. I'd see she ate the perfect collection of dishes. I'd see her smile at me as she smiled at him. And when eyes were averted, I'd see her on her knees under that white table cloth, sucking my cock for dessert.

I'd chose her underthings, her dress, the shade of her lipstick.

But first things first...

My angel declined a second glass of that atrocious wine, and from my shadowy corner, the corners of my lips turned up.

She had once given me the strangest and most appealing of compliments. My angel had claimed I had a dangerous smirk.

That's my girl.

Refined, poised, completely wasted working the counter of the chic local wine shop. Utterly too good for the filth talking with his mouth open across from her. But she didn't seem to grasp that. Smiling, attentive.

God... she looked happy.

Unacceptable.

Grinding teeth that had been expertly straightened by the best orthodontist money could buy, I felt a growl catch in my throat.

Fucking slut! Traitorous bitch!

My angel was lucky I had slaked my urges before I had left work on that insane menace. Lucky I had seen the blood-drained corpse of Mrs. Boyd and reveled in the sight before I showered, changed, and arrived *on fucking time*, to see her. How dare she look at any man but me in such a way!

I would carve these rules straight onto her ass if I must. Make sure she saw it in the mirror every goddamn time she was naked.

In the near future, she would only look at me. Only speak to me. No other. Ever.

A deep breath, blown out slowly between pursed lips

slowed my heart rate. Now was not the time for anger. My angel would face that later.

But I knew I'd go soft on her. How could I resist those eyes?

I'd hurt her, yes, but in a gentle manner. Lick her cunt, nibble her clitoris, finger her ass, and come down her silken throat. Teach her to relish the edge of pain in pleasure.

She would worship me.

And because I love her, I would expend my more aggressive tendencies on those at the asylum who deserved to be cowed.

I'd face fuck them, and then I would go home and make love to my wife.

I'd fuck their asses dry, then scrub clean of their madness and tend to my wife's every physical pleasure.

She would worship my cock.

The fucking lunatics would fear it.

The perfect balance of a man of my prowess and skill.

And that boy with her tonight. If he ever so much as looked at her again, by the time I was done with him, I'd hire five disease-riddled crackheads to expend their filth in his every orifice while I broadcasted it live on the internet.

Their main course arrived.

In five minutes flat, my angel's date had gluttonously cleared his plate. Standing to excuse himself for the restroom, he forgot to button his jacket. More importantly, she had not even eaten half of her pasta, and he thought it decent to leave her unattended.

Seeing her so slighted cooled my temper and made my arms ache to pull her to my chest and tell her what a good girl she was.

The best girl. My girl.

Corners of my mouth blotted, I set the pristine white napkin to my table and rose. Unlike the poor excuse for a man wasting her time, the top button of my jacket was closed. Shoulders back, smooth as silk, I too eased my way toward the men's room.

Couples paid me no mind, not when they were wrapped up in the ecstasies of their Valentine's dinner. Low conversation surrounded my easy walk to the hall where I'd end my angel's interest in this man.

The perfect day to stake my claim.

He was at the urinal, shriveled cock in hand. Head thrown back, Buck projected a loud sigh toward the ceiling. Letting it all out.

Pig.

Managing the criminally insane required more than a keen mind. It required a body honed and trained in take-down protocol. I knew just what kind of pressure to exert when my forearm circled Buck's throat. The expired jock thrashed, piss missing the porcelain and dribbling down his pants when I cut off his air.

Lucky for him, not a drop was splashed on me.

I would have cut his fucking throat if he'd ruined this suit. After all, I'd had it made in the very shade of gray she'd chosen to paint her bedroom walls. It complimented my tan skin. It fit like a glove. And it was hers. Just as I was.

I already had a long list of peasants who would be left in a shallow grave for speaking rudely to her at the store.

But this boy, this wriggly fish already going limp in my grip… I needed this piece of human filth to live.

A breathing example my angel would have to face.

Calm, the dulcet tone I worked over riled patients drifted from my lips to caress Buck's ear. "When you were fourteen you convinced your anorexic sister to suck your tiny cock. Told her you'd teach her what boys like and swore you'd make her popular like you."

Face going red, hardly able to speak, Buck grunted, "What the fuck, man?"

"What would the world think if they knew? How about if they knew about your love of animals? You don't even want to get me started on the horse cock plaguing your browser history. Tsk tsk, Buck. Not sure your buddies on the force would look so kindly at your love for donkey shows. You'd never get that dream job as a cop, Mr. Mall Security Guard, nor would you ever live it down. I'd make sure of that."

There it was, that fear all men had deep down when they were ripped open and exposed. He knew, the visceral animal part of him that brayed when he came down his sister's throat all those years ago knew every word I spoke was true. "What... do... you... want?"

This was where he'd offer me money, should I give him the opportunity. More money than he'd been willing to spend on my perfect angel's dinner.

"It's simple." My grip loosened just enough that I could assure he heard every last word that I snarled in his ear, yet remained tight enough he was on the cusp of passing out. "Leave. Now. Never so much as speak to Greta Larson again. No calls. No texts. Should she approach you in public, she does not exist."

"She's just some chick I want to fuck. I don't even know her!"

My future wife was so much more than this pig would ever know. "Your sister started cutting after you used her mouth. She never became popular like you promised."

"Jesus..." Buck's voice cracked.

My biceps once again bulging, I made sure his world began to spin. "When you wake up, take your piss soaked self out the back door. Disappear from Greta's life or yours will be this town's greatest laughing stock."

* * *

Had she not deserved the punishment, my heart would have ached at the scene of the manager approaching my angel an hour later to demand payment for her bill. Those minutes had stretched between us, her honey eyes shifting from glittering with excitement over a Valentine's date in our town's best restaurant to darting side to side with shame when Buck failed to return.

He'd already ordered them a chocolate soufflé. It takes at least thirty minutes to make, costs a small fortune as the chef makes the best in the state, and there it sat before her. Puffed, ready to be savored by a discerning palate.

Wasted.

A slow trickle of tears on her face had come long before management began to bark.

Humiliated was not a strong enough term for what she was going through.

I knew she could not afford to pay the bill. Her accounts I monitored daily. My darling angel gave the majority of her paycheck to cover her narcissistic mother's mortgage.

That cunt would be rotting in the ground by Christmas.

…though I'd make it seem natural and easy. After all, I didn't want my wife to mourn.

"Please… Buck will be right back, let me just call again. I'm sure he'll answer." That voice I loved with my whole being, that rich voice that sang of sex and longing while remaining somehow virginal and innocent, begged.

Breath pushed from my chest, I sighed. Yes, I knew such loud breathing was uncouth, but who could resist when their dearest was so undone?

She was in emotional pain.

She was publically mortified.

"I can… umm"—she fumbled for her grandmother's

watch, offering the dated thing as if it might be worth something. It wasn't—"maybe wash dishes? Please don't call the cops."

Oh, they would. And when they did, I'd call in a favor to a man whose mother I kept out of his hair.

The maître d' took her roughly by the elbow and hissed, so loud all could hear, "Others are waiting for this table."

In a day or two, I'd break his arm.

My angel began to cry in earnest. The kind of tears one tries to hold back so they come out so much louder. After a terribly cute hiccup, she confessed. "I can't afford the bill."

Oh, what a sap I was…

Standing, the broadness of my shoulders and the trim cut of my waist emphasized when I buttoned the top button of my jacket, I strode from the shadows and smirked just the way she liked. "Greta, what a pleasure seeing you here."

That delicious confusion on her face. How it blended with abject shame and made the tears ruining her mascara all the more beautiful. "Dr. Chaucer? I, umm… hello."

In the lightest of elegant reprimands, I said, "Rodney? Remove your hands from my friend. Can't you see she's upset?"

The snap, the way the peon jerked to attention at my call, I could not suppress the twinkle in my eye and let her see how I commanded the room. My darling angel, Greta, sucked her lush lower lip between her teeth in hope, in total remorse… in confused desire. All the room had turned to stare at the tableau, now they stared because the most eligible bachelor in town had come to smile at the impoverished beauty begging for reprieve after her date stood her up.

Spirit aglow with all that I knew would grow between us, I covertly ran a hand over the pocket that housed her engagement ring and gave her my full smile. "May I join you? It would seem my dinner partner never showed."

How I prized that angry, unguarded look in her eye on my behalf. In her mind, we two were kindred spirits trapped in the disappointment of the expectations of Valentine's evening. "I'm sorry, sir—"

Yes. She'd called me sir, and I was rock hard as I tossed Buck's slimy napkin aside and took his abandoned seat. I offered her the first boon between us. "Call me Fredrick."

"—but I am afraid I can't—"

"Never mind that." Hand waving the buzzing maître d' away, I offered as if it were nothing, "Put it on my tab."

"Dr. Chaucer—"

"I told you to call me Fredrick." That tone, it was the same I used with patients to give them their first warning. How it worked. Her shoulders snapped back, her pupils went to points, and Jesus, her nipples grew hard.

But not from desire.

This was something else. Something I would foster in her, break, and control.

"I'll order us a bottle of Opus One, 2013." That would have to do for her palate. My angel had yet to deserve her favored cab franc.

"That's a $500 bottle of wine!"

"And?" This temperament would not do. My future wife, my angel, must take what was given. Whether it be my throbbing dick down her throat, or a finely aged wine I'd been waiting to share with a kindred soul.

"Fredrick." She tested my given name on her tongue. "I... you don't have to do this."

But I did. I had to do everything for her. Always.

Such as chain her to my bed, fuck her until she learned to scream my name in delight. Kill her mother. Her former lovers, her irritating best friend.

That one would be my favorite. Lucy Bryant would be the first to go.

Not that I would do it myself.

No, I would watch the glory of that moment later on my phone, my bound and sated woman sleeping in my arms, my semen running out from between her battered thighs.

Lucy's murder would be perfect end to the perfect night.

ABOUT ADDISON CAIN

USA Today bestselling author &
Amazon Top 25 bestselling author

Addison Cain is best known for her dark romances, smoldering Omegaverse, and twisted alien worlds. Her antiheroes are not always redeemable, her lead females stand fierce, and nothing is ever as it seems.
Deep and sometimes heart wrenching, her books are not for the faint of heart. But they are just right for those who enjoy unapologetic bad boys, aggressive alphas, and a hint of violence in a kiss.

Join Addison's Facebook Reader Group!

Sign up for Addison's Newsletter.

ALSO BY ADDISON CAIN

Branded Captive

Wren can't sing like a bird. She can't speak at all. The Alpha kingpin
and his pack didn't buy the Omega to hear it talk.

The Golden Line

They call me brutal. They call me unrepentant. They call me
possessive. I am all these things and *much* worse. But to her, I will be
conqueror.

Dark Side of the Sun

Greedy, cunning, cruel, Gregory claims to love her, offers to kill for
her… but lies come easily to his tongue.

BECOMING

BY CELIA AARON

The curl doesn't lay quite right. I pick up the iron and re-wrap my hair around the hot rod and wait. Counting backwards from ten, I stare at the offending lock of hair in the mirror. Once I reach zero, I release the strands. The curl bounces along my shoulder. It's perfect. Because it looks just like *hers*.

I grab the next lock of hair and do the same, waiting the required ten seconds that it takes my hair—dyed to match *hers*—to act appropriately. I try to remember if she did a good job curling the back today. I don't think she did. So, I only give the strands in the back five seconds, and hold the iron a bit askew.

Curling my hair is a real pain, but Greta did it, so it only makes sense for me to do the same. Just like it makes sense for me to use her blush, highlighter, eyeshadow, eyeliner, and mascara. She just changed to the new Fenty foundation, which works pretty well on my skin. I wished she'd gotten something with more coverage, but of course she only bought what worked for her and her perfect skin tone. It took me weeks of bleaching my sun-damaged face to match her shade. Not to mention how hard it was to find contacts that matched the shade of her golden eyes. But, as I stare in the mirror, I realize it was worth it.

If she could see me, she'd probably think I was copying her. That I wanted to *be* her. Of course not. I laugh, my mouth quirking at one corner just like hers does. I know I'm better than her. I always have been.

I pluck a hair from the shoulder of my dress and toss it to the floor of her bathroom. The dress? It looks better on me. Just like everything of hers. All of it should be mine. Even that dope Buck Cummings who she's on a Valentine's date with right now. It's why she curled her hair and wore this dress. I know what you must be thinking, but give me a break. I just happen to have bought the exact same one. We have similar fashion. So similar that my closet could be hers. But it's not. It's *better*.

Am I jealous that she chose to go out with Buck instead of hanging with me for Valentine's? No. I only tolerate her presence. I don't enjoy it. Don't *crave* it. I can't let her know any of this, though, so I try to indulge in my habits when she's not around. But I can quit anytime I want.

I unplug the iron and carefully replace it on her vanity, then grab my phone. I open the tracking app and squint at the screen. (Greta has perfect vision and never has to squint at anything. That's because she's a spoiled cunt.) Where is she? I zoom in on the map. She's supposed to be at a restaurant with her date. She isn't. She's in a residential neighborhood in the ritzy area of town. Buck doesn't live there. I already researched him right down to his knockoff Calvin Kleins. No, she is somewhere she shouldn't be. Somewhere I don't know about. And I know every-fucking-thing about that bitch Greta.

This will not stand.

I flick through my contacts, then call Bradley.

"Yeah?" Greta's older brother answers on the second ring.

"Do you know where she is?"

He sighs low and heavy. "It's creepy the way you keep tabs on her, you know that?"

"Where is she?" I keep my tone even.

"It's Valentine's, Lucy. She's probably on a date. Like me. Let her have one night without you."

No. "So you don't know?"

"No, Lucy. Look, I gotta go. My date is waiting."

"Fine." I hang up with an angry finger stab at my screen. He can't help me—or maybe he *won't*. And I don't know what's going on. There's only one option.

I hurry into the hall and pull on my heels. It's important to note that these are not the same as Greta's. Hers are far more whorish and impractical and I would never wear them in a million years. Also, the store didn't have my size.

***

I park in front of a gothic-looking mansion straight out of a high-end horror flick nightmare. It even has gargoyles perched around the front entry. How did Greta end up here? The place must have cost millions, and then some asshole spent even more money to make it ugly. I would never understand rich people.

Closing the door to my car quietly, I edge up to the front door. It's wooden and heavy looking with a little glass porthole covered in an iron cage at eye-level. I peek through but can't see much of anything besides a dark entryway. No Greta.

A chill winter wind sweeps by and up my skirt. I wish Greta had thought to wear a jacket before she went out. Of course she didn't. So now I'm the one who has to pay the price. I wrap my arms around myself and step off the stoop.

Creeping around the house, I peer into each window I see, but the shadowy interior doesn't tell me anything except some stuffy rich asshole lives here.

I push through a fence to the back of the property. A well-manicured flower garden surrounds a sparkling pool. It steams a little in the moonlight, and the lounge chairs around it are arranged neatly at perfect angles.

A long row of windows span across the back of the house. I'm exposed, but I can't stop now. Not until I know what Greta is doing. I'm her best friend. It's my place to know. Just like it's my place to check her apartment for any changes each night as she sleeps. I hate her, but I'm also the only thing keeping her safe. *I'm* the one who decides when she isn't safe anymore. Her life hangs by *my* thread, no one else's. So why the hell is she somewhere she isn't supposed to be?

The back door beckons, the glass panes glinting in the light from the pool. I turn the handle. It doesn't move.

Fuck. I continue skirting the back of the house until the walls turn to that dark gray stone once more. Smaller windows appear at intervals. I check each one until I realize that whoever owns this house is a stickler for locks.

I circle back around to the wide windows near the pool. Out of options, I grab a stone from one of the planters and take aim at the back door, then stop. This is going to be so loud. I bite my lip in the way I've practiced for months—the same way Greta does it, her front teeth just barely pressing into her plump bottom lip. I hurry to the pool and snatch a cushion from one of the chairs, then go back to the door with the brick wrapped in the fabric. Kneeling, I smash the pillowed brick into the glass. It cracks but doesn't shatter. At least the sound is muffled.

Another hit sends a shower of glass into the house, the

tinkling noise shockingly loud to my ears. I stop, hold my breath, and wait for the lights to turn on or someone to come running. I count backward from ten, waiting for the scene to settle. When no one shows, I breathe again and knock a little more glass out of the way so I can open the door. It swings inward on silent hinges.

Rich wood floors spread out before me, and fancy furniture and art decorate the space. Though nice, the house has a distinctly masculine feel, right down to the leather upholstery. That slut Greta came home with some man—not even the one she was on the date with! All this time I'd believed her when she'd said she was a virgin. I even abstained from sex because of it. But no, she went home with a stranger. Goddamn whore. And where the fuck is she?

I creep around the glass and ease farther into the house. Something thumps above me, and I freeze. And then I hear it. Her voice in a high-pitched scream. I hesitate for a moment and quietly try to mimic it. But I can't quite hit the same note. Damn. I'll have to practice it, I suppose. The scream comes again, this time followed by the baritone of a man's voice.

I hurry through the downstairs, the empty feel of every room telling me that no one's home. Just the people upstairs. And one of those people belongs to me.

I find a wide stairway near the front door and creep upward like a cat. More thumps, another scream, and the man's voice grows louder.

"—everything for you, my pet."

She's crying now. I would be disgusted with her weakness if I weren't taking notes on just how her voice catches when she sobs. "P-please—"

"You are my perfection, the one I've been searching for. Submit to me, and everything you've ever wanted will be yours." He sounds reasonable to me. Too bad he's coveting my most prized possession.

I reach the landing and edge down the hall. It's decorated with even more art, the paintings growing darker and more macabre as I approach the closed door at the end. Greta would hate this décor. The bitch still hangs unicorn paintings in her house. Hell, the one I got her for Christmas is in her bedroom, the camera hidden in the horn and giving a perfect view of her while she sleeps.

"Your tears only excite me, my perfect one." His voice is raspy now, as if he's been exerting himself. "Look what you do to me."

"No, please don't hurt me anymore—"

"Look!"

Her whimpers send a jolt of delight through me. The only problem is that I'm not the one eliciting them.

I reach the door and turn the knob slowly. An agonizing amount of time goes by as I ease the door open millimeter by millimeter until I can see.

The room is huge with a bed against the far wall and a cage, some sort of leather horse thing, and a rack of whips and restraints in the center.

Greta is naked and on her knees, her hands tied behind her back. The man stands beside her, one of his hands stroking his hard cock, the other wrapped in her hair. He's familiar somehow, though I can't place him.

"Open your mouth. I want to feel that soft tongue." He sounds more angry than turned on – which makes my stomach clench and heat bloom between my thighs. It doesn't hurt that his body seems to be chiseled from some sort of unrelenting stone. He's a sick fuck, but a hot one.

She shakes her head and sobs some more.

"This is not how my future wife should behave." He wrenches her head back so she has to look up at him. "I gave you that ring as a promise. I promised my love, and you promised your obedience. And you are already breaking your vow!"

She screams as he pulls harder, bending her back at a painful angle.

I snap out of it. She's mine. Not his. And *no one* takes my toys away from me.

Shoving the door open, I step into the room.

He looks up, his eyes narrowing. "Lucy."

That's a surprise. He knows me. Perhaps I'm not the only one who's into watching.

"Let her go." I put my hands on my hips.

He loosens his hold on her, and she crumples to the floor in a blubbering heap. "She's mine."

The words are like acid on my ears, and a white-hot rage pulses through me. "Wrong, asshole. Greta belongs to *me*." I advance on him, my eyes going to the rack of implements. I snatch a long cane from it and brandish it in front of me.

He looks me up and down, his mouth twisting into a smirk. "The shoes are wrong. And your breasts don't fill out the top. Not like hers do."

"Lucy, run. Get help." Greta tries to crawl away.

"I can handle the situation." I don't take my eyes from the man. "And you are?"

"You can call me Dr. Chaucer." He darts forward and grabs a whip from the rack. "You know, I planned on taking care of you tonight, so I should be thanking you for showing up here and making my job easier."

"Go ahead then." I try to bend the cane between my hands. It has very little flex. Good. This will work perfectly on the good doctor. And what a stroke of luck to run into him tonight.

"Thank you." He gives a curt bow, then tests the whip

with a vicious crack. "Now if you'll come a little closer, I'll make it quick."

"Oh?" I circle around toward Greta. The dumb bitch hasn't gotten up to run yet.

"I'll use my hands." He follows my movements. "Wrap them around your throat. Squeeze until you stop writhing. You won't be the first insane woman I've killed. Not even the first of the day."

"Insane?" I cock my head to the side. "Excuse me?"

He laughs. "Just look at you, Lucy. Obsessive. Delusions of grandeur. Compulsions galore." He cracks the whip again. "I know all about you."

"I don't think so." I grin and reach down to pull Greta to her feet.

"What have I missed?" He advances.

I push Greta toward the door and put my back to her. "Run, Greta. I'll catch up."

She stumbles into the hallway.

"What have you missed? Plenty, Doc." I lash out with the cane and catch him on the side of his neck.

He roars and backs away. "What do you mean?"

"That had to hurt, eh?"

"Not as much as you're about to hurt." He rushes me, and the cane goes flying from my hand.

I sidestep, but he gets me around the waist with one arm and drives me to the floor. The back of my head cracks on the wood, and my vision blacks for a moment.

"You have *ruined* my perfect evening!" He climbs on top of me and clocks me hard on one cheek.

I laugh and buck up, throwing him sideways. I flip over and straddle him, then rain down punishment on his handsome face. Each hit fuels me, giving my rage a whole new life.

"She's mine. *Mine.*" I backhand him as he sputters, blood

running from his split lip.

With a growl he shoves me off, and we grapple until he gets a lucky break and pins me face down.

"You broke my nose, bitch." His words are slightly slurred.

"That's not all I'm going to break." I pull at his forearm as he tries to choke me out.

He lands a hard punch to my side that sends my breath wheezing out. "I was just going to kill you. But now you've pissed me off, stupid girl. You're going to get worse than a quick death." He reaches down and yanks up my skirt.

I struggle under his weight, but he manages to yank my panties down and jab his fingers between my legs.

He stills. "What the—"

I raise up with him on my back and drop, crushing him beneath me.

"Joke's on you, Doc." I roll over and kick hard into his side. My heel connects, and one of his ribs cracks.

He yells and curls into a ball. "A man. You're a—" His painful wheeze cuts off the rest.

"Lou." I grab him by the foot and drag him toward the bed. "Name's Lou. At least it was." I let my voice drop, the sweet tone I'd modeled after Greta's dying away into my baritone. "Until I met her."

"My angel."

I pick up the whip and use it to bind his hands. "Mine." I correct him. "She's mine. Not an angel, either. She torments me. And she'll keep tormenting me until I *become*."

"You copy everything she does—"

"No!" I kick him again, and this time his scream reaches some interesting pitches. "I don't *copy* her. I'm more than she ever could be. I am becoming."

"Becoming what? You're." He wheezes. "Insane."

"Is that your professional opinion?"

"Yes," he grunts.

I drag him to the handy cage, shove him inside, and click the lock in place. Then I back away and admire my handiwork. My face aches where he hit me, but I'm otherwise none the worse for wear.

I drop down to my haunches in a decidedly unladylike fashion. "Next time you should research a little more thoroughly. Especially when you decide to take a toy from a former UFC fighter."

Recognition finally fires in his eyes. "Lou Dantonio?"

My lips almost crack, I smile so big. "Remember me now?" I flex my fists. "I'm smaller now. Had some surgical changes to aid in my transformation. But I'm still the same bruiser you used to torture for fun when I was in the loony bin with you."

"I don't care who you are. I'll kill you for this. For taking her." The anguish in his tone is almost touching. "Angel!" he yells. "Come back to me sweet angel!" Turning to me, he snarls, "I already took her cherry. It'll never be yours."

"I never wanted it." I shrug. All that means is that I'm free to start tapping ass whenever I feel like it. "Thank you."

"If not that, then what do you want?" He looks genuinely confused.

"Her."

"Her what?" He shakes his head.

"All of her. I want to take everything she is and suck the fucking life out of it. I want to own her soul."

"That's—"

"Insane, right?" I wink at him. "I'm *becoming*, Doc. I don't expect you to understand. I'm already better, and when I take every last bit of her, I'll be superior in every way. Her life will end in these hands, not yours." I show him my palms.

A creak in the hall catches my attention, and I stand. "Greta." I adjust my pitch to a higher, softer note. Why the hell did she come back? She's a coward. Always has been. Weak. That's why I chose her.

Turning, I gawk. She has a gun. Where the hell did she even find it?

"Move aside, Lucy." Her voice wobbles, but she holds the pistol steady and aims at the cage.

"Are you going to—"

"Move." Still nude, she advances in the room.

I back away and stand at her side.

Dr. Chaucer sits up in the cage. "My angel. My perfect Valentine. Put the gun down. This isn't you. You are everything soft and feminine and beautiful. This isn't like you. You aren't—"

"You don't fucking know me!" She screams, and the pistol roars. Blood spurts from the doctor's chest, and his expression turns to utter shock as he stares down at the gushing crimson.

"Angel." He sputters. "My perfect angel. I love you. I love you so much." Blood spills from his mouth as he begins to cough.

"I'm not yours. I will *never* be yours." She fires again, and he goes down, his eyes open and staring as his life ends. Good. He got what he deserved for trying to steal from me.

She lowers the gun and wipes her face with one hand.

"Greta." I reach for her. "Give me the gun."

She turns on me, the pistol up again. "You think I'm stupid?"

"What?" My blood goes cold.

"You think I don't notice the way you copy everything about me?" She sniffles, but the gun doesn't waver. "The contacts, the hair, the clothes, all the way down to my fucking nail colors and the same way I wrinkle my nose when I laugh!"

I clear my throat. "I can explain all that—"

"I know. I just heard your explanation. You want to hurt me. Maybe even worse than he did." Her golden eyes harden, as if she's turning from putty to stone right before my eyes. It's a gut punch.

"No." I shake my head as a ringing starts in my head. "Don't do that."

She laughs, but it's a harsh sound, nothing like her usual musical tone. "Don't shoot you?"

"No, don't *become*. Stop." I put my hands to my ears and close my eyes. "I'm the one who is supposed to become, not *you*!" She's changing right in front of me, her back straightening, her soul coalescing into something born of fire and steel. I can't take it. Not now. All this work. All this effort. All for nothing.

"What the fuck are you talking about?" Her finger still rests on the trigger. "I thought you were harmless. I thought it was flattering. But it was sick the whole time. You're sick."

"Stop!" I scream as she changes, and Greta is gone. The Greta I could have used, the vessel, the one I would always be better than. All gone. Grief and hate mix inside me until they combust. I rush her, ready to destroy her rather than let her fully *become*.

The pistol flash is the last thing I see.

ABOUT CELIA AARON

USA Today Bestselling Author

Celia Aaron is a recovering attorney who loves romance. Dark to light, angsty to funny, real to fantasy--if it's hot and strikes her fancy, she writes it. Thanks for reading.

Join Celia's Facebook Reader Group!

MY BLOODY VALENTINE

BY SJ COLE

The clatter of dishes, the overly-smiley waiters, and the pop of champagne bottles annoys me to no end. Don't even get me started on the intermittent giggles of all the stupid, love-sick girls hanging on their date's every word.

Valentine's Day is a crock of shit. A day where single people feel sorry for themselves and those of us in relationships hold ridiculously high expectations.

Like me.

I had expectations for fucking Bradley to do something amazing. Epic. Romantic. Not bring me to this four-and-a-half-star joke of a restaurant.

I glance across the room at him. He shoots me an almost sexy smile, and there's a moment where I envision myself taking his head and slamming it against the table until his ruby-red blood splatters the starched, white tablecloth.

"Paige?"

Gwen's saccharin-sweet voice draws my attention away from Bradley.

"What are you staring at?"

"Nothing." I snag my glass of wine, grinning around the rim. Gwen would never understand that the reason I asked her to dinner on this shitty day was because of Bradley, not because she caught her two-timing skeeze of a boyfriend balls deep—again—in one of his secretaries.

My gaze strays back to Bradley, and my heart somersaults. Blond hair that's always perfectly styled, chiseled jaw. The way his slacks hug his ass should be considered a cardinal sin, and when he smiles—I clutch at my chest, yes, be still my heart—because when that man smiles, it's as though heaven has opened its gates and welcomed me into eternal salvation.

"What did you think of that patient?" Gwen asks, twirling a piece of hair around her finger.

"Which one?"

Her jaw slacks. "Mr. Bumpus." She said his name loud enough for the table beside us to hear. "You know he. . ." she rambles on and on about the poor man.

With a sigh, I drum my fingers over the white tablecloth while the HIPAA violations mount against my dear friend with every breath she takes. One day, someone will report her. Our Lady of Perpetual Sorrow Asylum takes patient privacy very seriously. As they should. How would society function if everyone's secrets were out in the open? Just think how paranoid people would be if they knew their jolly FedEx guy likes to cut off the flesh from inside his thigh and eat it.

Some things are better kept under wraps. People like me. Most certainly people like Bradley. Oh, Bradley. I try to focus on Gwen and the dull drone of her conversation, but my attention eventually drifts back to him. He's the sun, and I'm but a feeble planet caught in his orbit. My jaw clenches. That's not the way it should be. I should be the goddamn sun, and he should be the feeble speck of matter eternally bound to orbit in my glory. Bradley, I should punish you for making me feel so insignificant.

"What are you looking at?" Gwen turns in her chair then shakes her head. "You're off in La La Land tonight."

"I just thought I saw. . ." My words stick in my throat like molasses. And for a moment, I hope I choke on them and keel over right on this table because Bradley just stood and pulled out a chair for some skanky brunette. Oh, he gave her my smile when she swept her hair over her boney fucking shoulder. Red-hot anger batters my insides, my teeth grind together, but I somehow manage to keep it from bubbling over. Even though my pulse is throbbing in my neck and temples, I smile like the sweet person I am. "I thought I saw someone I knew. An old friend, but I don't think it's him."

"I hate when that happens. I'll stare and stare, kinda like you were doing, to the point of being creepy." Gwen rolls her hand in the air with a flourish before grabbing her wine glass and bringing it to her lips. "Nine times out of ten, if I say something to the person, it's never them, and then I just feel like an idiot." She giggles.

I giggle because I've learned that's the appropriate thing to do in situations such as these, situations where I do, in fact, think she's an idiot, but it would be frowned upon to say so.

The waiter steps to the table and places our meals in front of us. The aroma of roasted peppercorn and garlic lifts with the steam swirling from my filet. When I cut into the meat, blood seeps out and pools along the rim of the clean, white plate.

Throughout dinner, Gwen rambles about her life problems, bitching and moaning. I simply chew and agree with everything she says while I watch Bradley and Little Miss Perky Tits.

She flips her hair every few seconds. She laughs too much. And let's face it, Bradley, she's plain at best. All the other girls have been bombshells. Don't sell yourself short, sweetheart.

Gwen is in the middle of convincing herself she can do better than David, that she shouldn't give him a second chance, and I'm nodding like one of those stupid Bobbleheads when Little Miss Plain Jane Perky Tits gets up from the table.

I push up so fast my leg hits the table, rattling the dishes. Gwen's brow wrinkles.

"Where's the restroom?" I know where the restroom is because Bradley's whore is sauntering her way to it right now.

Gwen thumbs over her shoulder, and I grab my purse before hustling through the maze of lover-filled tables.

A warm buzz swims through my veins, nearly making me drunk as I think about how lucky I am that I'm a woman. Women get to take their purse everywhere without anyone questioning them. It makes life so much easier.

The door to the bathroom swings closed just as I come to it. I take a breath and steel myself when I notice the yellow sign in front of the employee's restroom. Restroom Closed. Fate is a very real force that is often on my side. Snatching the pretty little sign, I shove open the door and grin when I place it in front of the women's restroom.

Only one stall is closed, so I secure the lock. It's just me and Miss Tits. The trickle of piss echoes from the walls along with the click of my heels.

I go about setting my purse above the sink. I hum while I rummage through the tubes of slut-red lipstick and brown pill bottles until my fingers brush the smooth, plastic syringe.

The whoosh of the toilet sounds before the latch on the stall clicks, the hinges groan, and out she comes, hips just a swaying.

Leaning over the sink, I slather sheer gloss to my lips. She primps her hair.

A passing glance is exchanged, the kind that not only distracts her from the syringe concealed delicately in my clutched fist, but one that attempts to hide the fact that we're sizing one another up. Who's the prettiest, the slimmest? The most perfect for Bradley.

"That dress is gorgeous. Where'd you get it?" I ask, ever sincere.

It hangs off her lean frame like some cheap bargain basement curtain, but it would cling to my curves like a leather glove. Oh, I bet Bradley would salivate if he saw me strut out in that orchid-colored dress.

"This old thing?" She bats her fake eyelashes while I fight not to roll my eyes into next week. How drab must she be if she's actually using the: this old thing line. Bradley, I'm doing you a favor. I truly am. Consider me a martyr. "Van Maur," she says.

"It's stunning."

She dabs at a stray line of lipstick, then straightens the pearl pendant on her necklace before turning on her heels.

"Oh," I say, stepping beside her. I force a sugary smile because girls with sweet smiles are trustworthy. "You have something on your neck here."

Just like that, she sweeps that damn hair to the side, offering me the perfect spot. My soul tingles at the sight of her throbbing pulse. With practiced ease, I stab the needle into her throat and press the plunger.

She swats at me only once before her eyes roll back, and her knees buckle. Her head whacks the sink with a pleasing crack before her body crumples to the floor. Blood leaks from the gash in her forehead, finding its way to the tile. The way it creeps along the grout lines reminds me of the filet I had for dinner, and I must say, both the steak and Miss Tits untimely demise were executed to perfection.

The pros of being a nurse doctors like to fuck: they turn their head the other way when I take home a few goodies. Good pussy will silence any man.

And this scrawny brunette could have never been good pussy.

I squat, my ass hovering over the pooling blood while I check to see how visible the puncture hole is. Nearly non-existent. For all anyone would know, it's a mosquito bite at best.

Quickly, I unfasten the silver necklace from around her neck then place it around mine. I'll give it to him; Bradley has good taste. He may have outdone himself this year.

After admiring the way the pearl hangs along my neck-line, I hide the syringe in my purse, making a mental note to place it in the sharps container first thing in the morning. A quick wash of my hands and I'm stepping over her lifeless body and through the restroom door.

A check in the hallway to make sure no one sees when I move the sign back to its rightful place, and then I'm off with a bounce in my step.

The song "Don't Go Breaking My Heart" plays in the background. I don't intend to break Bradley's heart—make it stop? I certainly hope it doesn't come to that.

When I make my entrance into the dining room, Bradley's eyes hone in on me. I swear, there's a slight smirk playing at his perfect lips. He checks his watch. Oh, I know, Bradley. I know I've kept you waiting, and I promise I'll make up for that.

"Paige?" Gwen calls for me when I pass our table.

"I'll be right back." Bradley is waiting, after all.

When I step behind him, my heart thrums like the wings of a hummingbird. He's so perfect. His eyes drag over my body as I round the table, setting me on fire before I take a seat.

He blinks. I smile, wondering if he'll fuck me right here on this table or if he'll wait to get me home before he eats my pussy raw.

"So glad you showed up, darling." He shoves a piece of salmon in his mouth. Our gazes lock while he chews. "It is flattering when you take the initiative to follow me."

"Who was she, Bradley?"

"No one of importance."

"Bullshit."

A small grin kicks at the corners of his lips, and I swoon. What a predator he is with his magazine-spread-worthy, mega-watt smile. Not a hair out of place. Not a cufflink unpolished. Everything down to his neatly pressed shirt suggests he's safe.

"Now, darling, you know they aren't important until they're dead."

With a roll of my eyes, I gulp back Miss Tits' wine until the glass is empty. "And how important she must have been for you to bring her to dinner on Valentine's Day."

"Did you enjoy playing with your present?" A rough chuckle slips through his lips and reaches between my thighs like a wet tongue. It's borderline pathetic how easily he gets to me. He takes the bottle of wine and refills my glass. "Tell me, how did you kill this one?"

I should hate him for making me do the things he does, but the sad truth is, I enjoy it just as much as he does.

A shrill scream causes the restaurant to fall silent. Bradley's face beams which sends my heart into a flutter. A flurry of commotion ensues while the wait staff runs about, calling the paramedics and attempting to clear the hallway of Nosey Nancies.

"Is there a lot of blood?" Anticipation gleams his eyes.

"Only from where she hit her head."

"Ah, what a shame. Blood on Valentine's Day is so festive." His eyes taper when he reaches across the table to grip the pearl between his fingers. "Next year, I should get you diamonds."

ABOUT SJ COLE

Stevie J. Cole (writing as SJ Cole), a Goodreads Choice Award Finalist 2016, lives deep in the woods of Alabama with her sexy husband and two precious daughters. She has an obsession with penguins and English chocolate and is terrified of clowns.
Her solo books offer you all the feels you've come to love in a warm, pretty romance with happily ever afters, while her SJ Cole books and her co-authored books with LP Lovell take you on a thrilling ride of suspense and danger, sometimes with a nice little kick of love.

Join SJ's Facebook Reader Group!

ALSO BY SJ COLE

White Pawn

The game's not over until the king is dead.

Absolution

I became his sinner and he became my sin.

Bad

True Power is never held by good men.

FOOL FOR LOVE

BY JULIA SYKES

Stupid fucking cunt.

I take a breath and pinch my arm, like Dr. Chaucer taught me to do.

You're not a stupid fucking cunt. I correct the negative thought pattern with the little bite of pain, struggling to rewire my brain.

No matter how many times I pinch or cut, the self-effacing thoughts won't stop.

The pain is supposed to help me build my self-confidence by eliminating my obsessive, unbidden thoughts.

But the only respite I find in the pain is the catharsis of punishing myself for being a worthless idiot.

No wonder David is cheating on me with his secretary.

"I can totally do better than David," I lie. "I deserve better."

The platitude I desperately wish my friend would offer issues from my own lips, a pathetic plea for her to agree.

Paige nods absently, her emerald eyes cutting past me to stare over my shoulder as she smooths her honey brown hair needlessly. She's been doing that all night, preening and looking for a distraction.

And why shouldn't she? I can hear how inane I am with every chattered sentence, but I can't stop myself from trying to fill the conversational void. I need Paige to like me, to laugh at my jokes about David being a jerk. I need her to think I'm fun to hang out with, even if I am dealing with a cheating boyfriend on Valentine's Day.

I need her to believe I'm everything I'm not. I need her to think I deserve attention. Empathy. Love.

I crave her approval. Even the crumbs of affection David offers me would be preferable to Paige's obvious boredom.

"Isn't David just the worst?" I giggle, as though my pitiful life is hilarious.

Paige is still staring over my shoulder. She doesn't respond for a full three seconds.

Three seconds is all it takes to have my fingers twisting in my napkin, anxiety clawing at my gut.

Stupid fucking cunt.

Before I can pinch myself and correct the compulsive thought pattern, Paige shoots to her feet, the movement jarring enough that the dinner plates rattle against the table. I gawk at her, horrified that she's drawing negative attention to us in this sophisticated restaurant. I'm barely able to afford my dinner, but I'd quickly agreed to join Paige when she invited me, eager to please her.

"Where's the restroom?" she asks, loud enough for the neighboring table to hear.

Inwardly, I cringe at her crass behavior. It will reflect

poorly on me. I can feel strangers' eyes pricking at my skin, judging us.

Judging *me.*

My cheeks burn, and I jerk my thumb over my shoulder, gesturing in the direction of the bathroom.

She grabs her purse and rushes off, impatient to escape my whining about my cheating boyfriend.

She's gone for what feels like hours. Nervously, I pick at my pasta.

I'm sitting alone on Valentine's Day, eating the cheapest dish on the menu. The prickling on my skin escalates to a hundred bee stings, making my flesh itch and burn. Everyone can see how pathetic I am, how worthless.

My fists curl in my lap to prevent myself from raking my nails down my arms. There's no point. Nothing will ease the physical manifestation of the strangers' judgmental stares. Their disapproval presses against my chest, making it difficult to draw breath in a normal rhythm.

Paige finally returns. I sigh my relief.

She walks straight past our table.

"Paige?" I call after her, struggling to keep the desperate rasp from my tone.

"I'll be right back." She waves at me in dismissal, not even sparing a glance in my direction.

I turn in my chair, watching her walk away. She slides into an empty seat across from a handsome man with blond hair and a chiseled jaw. He grins at her, and my heart stutters.

He was expecting her.

She had arranged a date with this gorgeous man.

She'd always planned to abandon me here.

And why shouldn't she?

I'm boring. Tedious. Plain.

Stupid fucking cunt.

"Gwen?" I jolt at the sound of my name in that familiar baritone.

Dread pools in my gut, and I tear my attention from Paige, my gaze lifting to find David's soft, blue jean eyes. His full lips tilt at one corner, twitching in a smirk. He quickly smothers it, arranging his angular features into something sympathetic.

"Are you here by yourself?" David asks.

"No!" I declare, a bit too vehement.

Those soft, sweet blue eyes scan the room, making a full circuit before coming to rest on my face. I feel myself shrink beneath the weight of his pitying stare.

"You don't have to lie, Gwen," he says, his rich voice smooth and soothing.

His lips twitch at the corner again. He glances down at my cheap pasta dish.

"Let me buy you dinner, at least," he offers.

My jaw drops. Did he come here to surprise me? Does he still want me?

I'm suddenly grateful that Paige abandoned me. It leaves me free to spend the evening with David.

"You know you can't afford this place," he tells me. The insult comes out like the gentlest rebuke. Like he actually gives a shit about my financial situation and wants to help me.

Warmth suffuses my chest. This is how he treated me in the beginning. He doted on me. He bought me expensive gifts and promised he'd always take care of me. He even invited me to live with him in his fancy house, rescuing me from my crappy apartment.

Now, he's here to woo me again. He's here to apologize for his mistakes and win me back.

He loves me. He wants me.

I'm worthy.

Relief rips through my system with visceral force, my heart expanding against my ribcage. I'm so full of love, I think I'll explode.

I beam up at him, sure my gratitude is glowing on my cheeks and shining from my eyes. I can't contain it within my own skin. "Thanks. I'd love that."

"David. There you are," a new, feminine voice purrs. A beautiful, willowy blonde appears at David's side. She clasps his hand in hers, perfect red-manicured nails curling around his fingers. Her dark chocolate eyes turn on me, and she doesn't bother to hide her smirk. "Gwen. It's so nice to see you."

My mouth opens and closes, my stare fixed on their intertwined hands. David caresses hers, running his thumb over the backs of her knuckles.

The same way he used to hold *my* hand. That sweet little gesture conveyed so much affection that it validated my existence.

Sarah Jennings' golden skin practically glows under the restaurant's romantic lighting, exuding glamourous perfection I'll never attain.

It's no wonder David has chosen his gorgeous secretary over me. How could I compete? My brown hair is mousy, my lips too thin to appear sultry. I don't wear makeup to work, and long, tiring hours at the asylum don't help my appearance by the time I return home every day. I'm lucky David deigns to fuck me. Lucky he lets me live in his house. Lucky he chooses to acknowledge me at all.

"You're…" I fumble over my words. "You're here together? On Valentine's Day?" I ask on a squeak.

Of course they are. He's holding her hand. Right in front of me.

We haven't even officially broken up. Just because I

caught him fucking Sarah in our bed doesn't mean I'm going to leave him, no matter what I'd said to Paige.

I don't deserve better than David. I never will.

"Don't be dramatic, Gwen," David admonishes in exasperated tones.

"I'm not," I insist like a petulant child. I'm defensive, as though I've been caught doing something I shouldn't. My face is hot with shame.

"There's no need to be immature," he says, pinning me in place with a paternal, disapproving stare. "We're all adults here."

"We should go to our table." Sarah tugs at his hand. She's not looking at me anymore. Her eyes cut to the side, color showing on her cheeks even through her thickly-applied bronzer.

I'm embarrassing her.

I'm embarrassing David. I can see it in the darkness of his gaze, the downward twist of those perfect lips.

"I'm sorry," I say, my voice small. "I'll just leave."

I get to my feet, preparing to flee from the awful situation.

"You're going to leave without paying for your meal?" David asks, the words dripping with disdain.

"I thought you said you'd…" I trail off and swallow against the lump in my throat. Mortification burns through my veins.

Stupid fucking cunt.

I can't expect David to pay for my meal when he's here on a date with another woman.

He lets out a heavy sigh. "I'll cover your bill," he offers, resigned. "You should probably go home. You look tired."

My eyes sting. I put on makeup and a pretty dress and everything, and I still look like shit.

No wonder he's chosen to fuck Sarah. I can't blame him. Even now, he's only trying to take care of me. He's paying for my dinner and telling me to get some rest at home.

Our home.

He still wants me, I reason. He wouldn't be telling me to go back to the house if he didn't want me.

"Thank you," I choke out before turning on my high heels and rushing away.

The stinging in my eyes intensifies, and I feel wetness pooling against my lashes. I hastily blink it away.

Lock your shit up, I order myself.

I've already made enough of a scene. I've embarrassed David and myself.

I manage to get out of the restaurant and into my cherry red sedan.

Well, it's not really mine. David bought it for me. I'm lucky he lets me drive his fancy, new car. I'm lucky he lets me live in his huge house in a pretty, safe neighborhood.

I'm so fortunate that he does all these kind things to protect me and take care of me.

I wish I could be worthy of his generosity. I wish I could be worthy of *him.* If I were, I'd be the one having dinner with him on Valentine's Day, not Sarah.

I drive to his house, berating myself with each breath.

Stupid fucking cunt. Stupid fucking cunt.

By the time I step through the front door and lock it behind me, I'm completely wound up, yet exhausted deep in my bones.

You look tired. David's concerned words ring through my mind.

Yes, I need rest. My body feels heavy, but my brain is buzzing. I'll make some chamomile tea to calm my nerves so I can sleep.

I trudge across the foyer, making my way through the enormous, open-plan dining room to get to the kitchen. I pause beside the dining table. I haven't bothered to turn on the lights, but I can see a shiny red package glinting in the moonlight that filters through the huge picture window.

My heart lifts, and a silly grin splits my lips as a sob rips its way up my throat.

David didn't forget about me. He got me a present for Valentine's Day.

My hands shake as I pick up the small package. It fits in the palm of my hand, so pretty in its romantic red paper. I tear away the wrapping, my fingernails scrabbling at the tape. I lift the lid on the little green box. A gorgeous, pear shaped diamond pendant glitters against black velvet.

I brush my fingers over the breathtaking gemstone, which is set in gold.

"Oh, David," I sigh into the darkness. "I love you, too."

My fingers are still trembling, but I handle the delicate necklace carefully as I remove it from the box. It takes a few tries to get the clasp to fix at my nape, but I'm determined.

A wicked thought blooms in my mind. I should greet David when he comes home, wearing this necklace. And nothing else.

As I strip off my clothes, I fantasize about getting on my knees and sucking his big, perfect cock.

How long will he be at dinner?

I shake off the thought of him sharing a candlelit meal with Sarah.

He's coming home to *me*. I can wait as long as I have to for the man I love.

When I'm fully naked, I glance around the room, trying to decide where is best to position myself. I want to look beautiful when he arrives, enticing. I've been regulating my diet for him, so I won't have to worry about any fat rolls if I sit in one of the chairs. I'm so grateful he chooses my food for me. He only wants me to be healthy.

He cares about me, and I love him so much. I couldn't live without him.

The dining room won't do for the scene I want to create for him. I'll light a romantic fire and settle down in his favorite armchair beside the fireplace.

My decision made, I take a step in the direction of the living room. Something gold catches in the moonlight out of the corner of my eye. I blink and look back at the dining table. A metallic envelope gleams against the polished hardwood.

David got me a card *and* a necklace.

Idly, I pet the pendant at my throat, stroking it with reverence. With my free hand, I reach for the envelope. I open this with more care than when I tore at the package. I'm calmer now, my nerves soothed by the pretty gift David bought for me.

The card inside is covered in rhinestone hearts, flashy and special. I open it, eager to see what sweet sentiment David has chosen just for me.

Sarah,

I couldn't find a jewel as beautiful as you are.

I hope this diamond will do.

Happy Valentine's Day,

David

I stare at the words. The first time I peruse them, my mind skips over the greeting. I read them again and again, but the growing weight in my gut compels me to acknowledge her name.

Sarah

Sarah

Sarah

Stupid fucking cunt.

How could I ever think this necklace is for me? I'm far too plain to deserve something so beautiful. Sarah is stunning, perfect. No matter how much I diet or how enthusiastically I suck David's cock, I'll never be good enough for him. I'll never be worthy.

The card drops from my numb fingers, and I walk into the living room in a daze. I plop down in David's chair by the fire. It smells like leather and like *him*, that sexy, purely masculine scent I can never quite define.

I draw my knees up to my chest, curling into the fetal position as tears track down my cheeks. I hold the necklace, rubbing the expensive gemstone between my thumb and forefinger.

I squeeze my eyes shut as the familiar, self-loathing litany runs through my mind, overtaking all my thoughts. It fills my head in a shrill scream: *stupid fucking cunt!*

The latch on the front door disengages, shocking me out of my despondent state. I never turned on the lights, but I recognize David's dark silhouette in the foyer. He's alone.

"Gwen?" he calls out into the darkness.

"In here," I croak.

He turns toward me, crossing into the living room and flipping on the light. My too-pale skin is illuminated, shining blinding white.

"What the fuck are you doing?" he demands, gesturing at my huddled, naked body. "You have mascara all over your face," he sneers. "You look like shit."

"Why don't you love me?" The question rushes out on a sob.

He barks out a cold laugh and walks toward me. "You're so insecure," he accuses. "It's a very unattractive quality."

He stops when he's looming over me, his blue eyes glinting and his pretty lips curved. He reaches for his belt.

The tinkling sound of the buckle makes me shudder, and heat pools between my legs.

My nerves are raw and my face is a mess, but I still want him.

"I love you more than anything," I confess. "I couldn't live without you, David."

He rolls his eyes. "Don't act so needy. You're killing my hard-on."

"Sorry," I whisper as he begins to stroke himself. I unfurl my legs from where they've been drawn up to my chest. Before I can get on my knees, he grabs my elbow, yanking me to my feet. His fingers dig into my flesh, hard enough to bruise. Wetness drips between my labia, my desire coating my sex, preparing my body for him.

He glowers at my throat. "What the fuck, Gwen?" he demands. His fingers close around the diamond pendant, and he rips it from my neck. The delicate gold chain bites into my skin before it snaps.

A soft cry of loss knifes from my chest.

He holds his fist up to my face, a threat and a taunt; the glittering gemstone dangles between his fingers.

"This isn't for you," he growls. "Why do you always ruin everything?"

"I'm sorry," I gasp. "I'll do better. I'll be better. I love you." My eyes fix on the diamond. It swings back and forth like a pendulum, entrancing me. "Don't you... Don't you love me?" The beseeching question leaves me on the barest whisper.

He chuckles, a cruel sound devoid of any warmth. "Love you? How could I ever love you? You're just a stupid fucking cunt. How many times do I have to tell you?"

"Don't say that," I beg. "Please, don't."

He laughs. "You can pretend for everyone else all you like, but I know what you are. You're nothing, Gwen. Of course you can't live without me. You couldn't function by yourself, because you're just a stupid fucking cunt. Isn't that right? Tell me."

I cringe. He's never made me say the words aloud before. "Please, David."

His grip firms on my arm, hurting me. Just like I deserve.

"Say it," he hisses.

"I'm a...I'm a stupid fucking cunt."

"Louder."

"I'm a stupid fucking cunt," I say clearly, meeting him square in the eye. Something breaks open in my chest, a dam I've constructed in my soul to hold in all the dark things. Every cruel word, every strike of his hand—I swallowed it all down, burying it deep and internalizing it.

But now, David has set me free.

I don't have to pretend I'm worthy anymore. I don't have to practice and preen and pray for scraps of affection.

There's no point. I can't change what I am.

A delighted giggle bubbles from my chest. "I'm a stupid fucking cunt."

I'll never be worthy of David's love. Why have I been trying for so long when I'll never be good enough?

I can't be with David. The very idea is laughable.

I reach behind me and find the cool, iron handle of the fire poker. I have half a second to register David's gorgeous eyes widening with surprise before I swing it at his head. The prong drives into his brain. His full lips part, his mouth dropping open. His eyes go blank. I rip the poker out of his skull. His muscular body drops to the floor with a dull thud. I draw back the iron bar again and swing it in a downward arc.

"Stupid fucking cunt! Stupid fucking cunt!" I shriek the words with each blow, his skull crunching beneath the weight of the metal prongs. His beautiful face is ruined, a gory mess.

Finally, I stop pulverizing his brain. I stare down at the lump of flesh that used to be David.

"Stupid fucking cunt," I breathe, the words leaving me for the last time. They're purged from my soul, along with all the dark things I've kept locked in my heart.

I'm just Gwen now, and I am enough.

ABOUT JULIA SYKES

USA Today bestselling author of dark and dirty romance.

She has always kept dark stories tucked away in her mind, so she was thrilled when she discovered that other people actually want to read them. Her books blend romance, suspense, and BDSM.

Join Julia's Facebook Reader Group!

Sign up for Julia's Newsletter.

CHILLING SEDUCTION

BY JANE HENRY

They say women swoon for men in uniform, but hell, give me a white lab coat. Power. Prestige. The ability to manipulate life and death. I always thought I'd look damn good a white lab coat and I have to admit, I do. The stolen name badge is the finishing touch.

I stand a little too long admiring how I look in this, and give my vision a half-smile.

Paige will lose her mind. She has a bit of a medical fetish. Tonight, I'll fuck her with the white lab coat on.

After I do what I came here to do.

She doesn't know what I'm planning.

I step into the hall and keep my eyes cast down. With my coat and name badge, I'll fit in here, but I can't make eye contact with anyone who might see through the thin disguise.

"Hello, doctor." Paige's low, seductive voice comes to my

left and my pulse spikes. I turn to her and gather her in my arms, pulling her to my chest before I give her a kiss that makes her eyes flutter shut.

"Bradley," she murmurs against my ear.

I lift up the hem of her scrub top and graze the underside of her full breast, the silky feel of her bra making my dick go hard.

"You're too good to me," I say, playing the hand I need to. She comes unhinged a tad too easily for my personal tastes, but I know how to handle her. "I hope that doctor you were talking earlier didn't get too friendly with you, did he?"

"No," she breathes, when my thumb traces her nipple, grinding her hips against my leg. Wanton little slut. "Never. I wouldn't let him."

Paige can be a ruthless bitch when she needs to be, but for me, she's putty in my hands.

"Good," I approve, giving her what she wants. "I'd hate to have to break his scrawny neck."

She practically giggles.

"Such a good girl," I croon in her ear. I take her lobe between my teeth and bite, eliciting a moan. "Now go finish your shift, and meet me at my place when you're through. Understood?"

She nods, breathless, her eyes half-lidded.

Dropping my voice, I issue a command in her ear, just the way she likes it. "Be on time tonight, Paige. If you're late, I may have to punish you." I tug a strand of her hair. "You remember last time what happened when you were a bad girl."

"Yes, doctor," she says with a breathy laugh, before she pulls away. I send her off with a teasing slap to her ass that makes her bite her lip.

It's almost too easy. She's already wet for me and I hardly even tried.

I watch her leave, then wait until she's gone before I make my move.

Turning back to the elevator, I push the button, and when it opens, quickly step in and press the button to the ground floor. I slide the access card she stole for me through the security slot. My pulse races when the green strip of light granting me permission to access the floor lights up. The elevator door swings shut and the carriage swoops downward. I stand erect. Should anyone see me, I belong here. But no one does.

The doors to the elevator swing open. I'm alone here. It's almost as if it were meant to be. The halls are vacant, and the woman I'm after waits for me. Quietly. Silently. Like the patient lover that she is, with none of the heated fucking passion I get from Paige.

The hall is stifling hot, and I run my finger along my collar to give me some relief. I always hated the heat. I'm suffocating under it, my lungs constricted as if I'm descending into hell itself.

But where she lies in wait is cool. Refreshing. Like lemonade on a summer day. Ice floating in a glass of whiskey.

I always liked the cold.

I walk noiselessly down the hall when I arrive at the right door.

Her door.

I've been here so many times, I've memorized it. The little nick on the bottom left corner. The scratch just below the doorknob. The sound it makes when the lock unlatches. Anticipation curls in my gut like smoke rising from embers.

I take out my access card and glide it through the security slot again. The green light makes my cock harden like goddamn fucking foreplay. My hands shake on the knob. It's been too long. I've been jacking off in the shower just thinking about this, and now my time has come.

When I open the door, the blissfully cool air washes over me like balm, and I fill my lungs with a contented sigh. She lies in wait like I knew she would. My gorgeous, perfect angel for the night.

I go to her, and shut out every other detail in the room but her faultless, beautiful body waiting for me. She almost looks like she's asleep, but for her open eyes.

"You look lovely tonight," I tell her, bending down to stroke her silken red hair, so striking against her pale skin. I love when they're like this. Their bodies perfectly molded to mine while I touch every curve and dip of their skin, uninhibited by silly protests and useless chatter. The essence of eternity hangs between us as I run my thumb down the side of her cheek and cup her jaw. I drop a kiss to her temple and savor this moment.

Utter flawlessness.

I take my time smoothing my hand over her arms, loving the way her cool skin molds to my touch.

I whisper in her ear, telling her what a good girl she is and how I can't wait to fuck her, to mark her.

No other man will ever touch her after me.

She's mine for tonight.

Forever.

Removing my jacket, I toss it to the side, shivering when the cool hair hits my skin. I fucking live for this. Adrenaline courses through my veins like I'm about to step into the boxing ring. My fingers shake with the urgency of the moment, as I remove my clothes. My cock, hard as steel, springs free from my boxers and I fist it, groaning while I take in her gorgeous form. Waiting for me. She'll wait forever, and hell if that doesn't make my balls ache to fuck her.

My cock swells in my hand as I remember what it was like with her before. Such a pretty girl, she almost looked wholesome, with her pale skin and wide eyes, wearing simple yet beautiful clothes. No one knew how much she begged to wrap her lips around my cock and swallow every drop of my come down the perfect column of her throat. How she bent over and begged me to fuck her ass, but not until I'd made her cry by hurting her. She was as fucked up as I am, and I'll miss that about her.

I sigh, closing my eyes, remembering the beautiful way she gave head like I was a god she worshipped. I pump my cock harder, faster, reveling in the memory of warm lips and wicked tongue, how she licked and teased and I'd choke her with my cock until her eyes watered. She loved when I did that.

I throw my head back, imagining her sweet cunt, soaked and primed for my cock. I can't stop my fist from pumping at the beautiful, erotic memory.

In my mind's eye, we're together again in tangled sheets. Touching. Grazing. Licking. Worshipping. I pay homage to her memory before I touch her.

How I used to straddle her and palm her wrists, so small and helpless in my hands. Everything about her was so fragile, so helpless, I groan out loud and tug my cock harder, my hips jerking involuntarily.

It's quiet. So quiet, I easily fall into the memory of my cock between her thighs, while I groaned in her ear. Somehow, knowing that her life would end so soon made the way I fucked her poignant and memorable. I drag this out, fully intending on fucking her gorgeous body one last time, but I'm so ready to come, I can't stop the frantic jerking.

I need to remember every fucking detail of this before I take her this one last time.

Lips parted just so, as if holding her breath in anticipation. Light glinting off her porcelain, unblemished skin. Full breasts begging for my palm. She used to love her nipples suckled. I swallow hard, slowing the jerky movements so I can savor this blissful moment.

I need to fuck her, need to the feel of her cool body sculpted to mine. My eyes go half lidded, the silent room filled with the sound of my rasping groans moments before I come, splashing on the cool, clean floor.

When I come down for the momentary loss of control, I get my shit together. I can go all fucking night, and it won't take long before I'm ready to mount her.

Some women say they want to be used and taken. Degraded. Abused. Owned.

They lie.

Degradation comes with a price. They want to...*cuddle* and shit. Talk. Share my bed. There's a price tag that comes with fucking any woman.

But not with her.

I walk to her slowly, anticipation making my cock swell again with need, but my glee is tinged with sadness. Our perfect night will end with finality.

There will be no more late-night trysts. Not with her.

The next time I come, it will be with another woman.

But this one was special.

A noise outside the hall makes me freeze.

Jesus.

I had to jerk myself off like a fucking teenager.

Have I missed my chance?

I brace myself to meet someone in the hall when I open the door, but see no one. I notice the light in the hall is dimmed, though, and I frown.

Has someone come down here? I look, and nearly jump out of my skin when Paige's voice arrests me.

"Bradley," she says, with chilling calm, like a mother scolding a child caught red-handed, "what were you doing in the morgue?"

She stands to the left of the door with her arms crossed on her chest, her eyes meeting mine with furious accusation. I recognize the glint in her eyes, the same fire she gets before she murders someone.

Paige knows exactly what I was planning on doing in the morgue.

I've seen her end the life of seven women I seduced for her, and up until now she's believed I enjoyed the game of cat and mouse and her undying devotion. She didn't care what happened to their lifeless bodies after they died.

But to me, it was all I cared about.

It isn't devotion in life I crave, but in death.

Women are fickle creatures. Impetuous. Flighty.

So much more complacent when the blood lies cold in their veins.

And as Paige looks from me to the door of the morgue, I know.

Paige knows I betrayed her. She knows I've used her to fuel my fetish.

The realization hits us both at once. She screams with maniacal fury before she lunges, the momentary fury my only warning.

I sidestep her so her body propels into the hall. Her arms flail just before her head slams into the wall. She howls and crumples to the floor before I make my move.

With almost effortless ease, I lift her body in my arms and hold her to my chest so she faces away from me, one arm restraining her last attempt to escape, my vice-like grip immobilizing her arms. I'm much bigger than she is, and I'm experienced in restraining her.

With one quick tug, I lift the stethoscope that still hangs from her neck, and with my right hand I wrap it tightly. I pull.

"Thank you for all you've done," I whisper in her ear, as

she flails and squirms, desperate for air, riddled with panic as I strangle the life out of her. But my hold on her is way too strong. It's almost laughably easy to strangle her, but I still make sure I do a thorough job of it.

She slumps against me, lifeless, but I hold the stethoscope in place for a full minute to ensure I've done my job and eased her into the darkness of death.

Finally, I let her go, sliding her limp body to the ground. I check her pulse. The red marks of the stethoscope on her neck are beautiful, the scars of her final struggle on earth.

My cock hardens when no pulse quickens beneath my fingers.

Paige is dead.

I swallow the lump in my throat.

This wasn't how I planned it, but hell, I've just been handed a fucking gift, as if fate herself orchestrated this turn of events.

Standing, I carry her in my arms back to the place of seduction, my sanctuary. Opening the door, I find a vacant bed for her. I strip her and lie her down on the cool metal as if I'm laying a sacrifice on an altar. I bow my head, the moment sacred.

Her body's too warm still, but within hours, she'll be ready.

Tucking a sheet over her, I kiss her still-warm lips.

I'll take my time.

Then tonight, I'll give Paige her final send-off.

ABOUT JANE HENRY

**USA Today bestselling Author
& Amazon Top 100 Author**

Jane Henry pens stern but loving alpha heroes, feisty
heroines, and emotion-driven happily-ever-afters. Her books
are sometimes dark, sometimes sweet, but always kinky.

Join Jane's Facebook Reader Group!

Sign up for Jane's Newsletter.

ALSO BY JANE HENRY

Island Captive: A Dark Romance

I was hired to apprehend a monster, a Dom sentenced to life for murdering his submissive. But when our plane crashes, we are the only survivors. Now I'm the one pursued.

The Bratva's Baby: A Dark Mafia Romance (Wicked Doms)

My orders were simple: Capture her. Marry her. Take her inheritance. Get rid of her. The bookish little recluse is worth more than she knows. And now she's mine.

Deliverance (NYC Doms)

He's bred to protect, and he has his eyes on me. Accidentally keying the car of a dominant may not have been my smartest move.

ALL WRAPPED UP IN A BOW

BY ASHLEIGH GIANNOCCARO

My phone won't stop buzzing in the pocket of my bloodied pants. I fish it out with my sticky fingers, making it hard to swipe on the glass screen. I haven't even bothered to go wash off, I just want to get this over and done with. I thought it would take longer. In a way, I was unprepared for her to lose it so soon. The doctor said it can take months for them to become that desperate.

"What, Sarah?" I sigh into the phone as I continue to fill out the tedious forms that come with the death of a spouse. "I really can't talk right now," I whisper so the orderly behind the desk can't hear what I am saying.

"Jack, I think something went wrong." Her voice cracks with the threat of tears. How does she already know? "I know you're with your wife, it's Valentine's, I'm so sorry. But, David went into his house and left me in the car. He left my gift at home, he wanted to stop and get it on the way to my place." She's rambling and I don't have time to listen to her shit now.

"I really can't, Sarah. Julia passed away this evening. I have things to do." I turn my back to the counter and see the way my bloody footprints have made a path down the shitty linoleum floor from her room to the nurses station and waiting area. A trail of my guilt, it follows me, a bloody shadow.

"Jack, I'm so sorry. I'm sorry." *She's not sorry, I'm certainly not sorry. I am ecstatic.*

"Why are you sorry?" I ask her. "This is what we wanted."

"I know. I'm sorry I bothered you, but Gwen just came running down the street covered in blood, stark fucking naked. I'm afraid to go inside, and David hasn't come out. Your sister has finally lost her shit, why do you two always protect her?" Ah, Gwen, the real whack job in this plan. Why my mother didn't drown her as a baby I will never understand.

"Call a cab, go home. Do not go inside. I'll have Gwen dealt with." *Fuck me, did it all have to happen on one night?* "I'll see you at the house later." I hang up and sign the bottom of the form allowing for Julia to be cremated as soon as possible and her ashes sent to me. There is no grief, no sadness, only relief — I am glad to be rid of my crazy fucking wife.

"Is Dr Chaucer in this evening?"

"No. I'm sorry, sir. He had a date for Valentine's, can I help you?"

"My sister, I think she's done something wrong. The neighbor says she just ran down the street naked and covered in blood. She was at home with my brother, he looks after her." I pocket my phone and place the clipboard back on the counter. "She's had problems before, she was a patient of Dr Chaucer's and I think she may need to be brought in."

"Do you have an address, sir? I will alert the authorities

and they can bring her here if she's found." I rattle off David's address and silently hope she did a proper job and he's dead, I don't need a pissed off brother, and a dead wife. *Both need to be dead.* He makes a nine-one-one call and stays on line with the operator while firing off questions to me. I hope Sarah gets the fuck out of there, quickly.

"I'm worried my brother may have been hurt," I lie through my teeth.

"Don't worry sir, the police are on their way." Police, I should be concerned about that. No one is going to come after a grieving man. I remember my wife is dead, and summon all the fake tears I can muster and sniff out.

"It's been an awful night, I can't take much more." A chubby nurse with faded scrubs comes and puts her arm around me, guiding me to chair in the waiting area. "Sit, we will take care of everything for you. I'm going to go find a doctor, and let him know Gwen is coming in. I saw one down by the morgue earlier." She scuttles off. I have to bite my tongue, because I know there's no doctor by the morgue. My heart skips a beat at who is down there, and I fight hard not to smile. *I'm grieving.*

I watch as a cleaner mops up the remnants of my wife off the floor, it's quiet inside my head. I don't hear the noise behind the desk, or the shouting of madmen behind doors. The mop turns from dirty grey to red as they clean the crimson splatters off the floor. Her blood is dried on my hands, and clothes now, the stickiness has gone. *Left me, like her life left her.* The doors swing open as a gurney is hurtled through the door.

Gwen's shrill screams break the silence I was so enjoying. She is tied down, restrained. Naked and bloodied from head to toe. Oh, she did a good job — clever girl. Look at all that blood, and the bagged fire poker in the EMT's hand is a beautiful confirmation that David will no longer be a problem. *For any of us.*

"What happened?" I put on the mask of concerned relative. "Where's my brother? What did you do, Gwen?" She screams louder now. They allow me to get close enough to see the insanity in her feral eyes. She can't even focus, she thrashes and pulls against the restraints.

"Sir, we need to get her into a room and sedated," The imposter doctor says, not letting on that we are already familiar. "The officer would like a word, then we will take you to see her. You are family?"

"Yes, we are family. She's my sister." I nod, wondering if I look bereft enough? The heavy-set police officer stands waiting for me. I make eye contact and hope he sees a sad, grief-stricken husband.

"Mr. Boyd."

"Call me Jack," I say, slumping down into the uncomfortable plastic covered waiting chair again.

"Jack, is David Boyd your brother?" I nod, watching his discomfort as he has to deliver bad news to me. "Sir, I understand you have already had a bad night, but I have to inform you that your brother was murdered earlier this evening. Gwen, your — um, sister, has confessed to us. You told the hospital a neighbor called you?" I nod again. Talking might tell him things I don't want to say.

"Yes. Okay, sir. We will need a statement and those details form you, sir."

"Officer, I have just lost my wife and my brother in one night. My sister has finally gone completely mad, and I am going to have to have her committed. So with all due respect, could I please do this in the morning? I would like to see Gwen, and then go home." Tugging at his collar, I can see he is uncomfortable in here.

"Sure thing, Mr. Boyd. Here's my card. You can pop down

to the station tomorrow. Or call me and I will come to you."
He looks around the empty room and then at the state of me.
"Is there someone to drive you home, sir? Do you want to
call someone or I can give you a lift?"

"I'll call someone from my office to fetch me. Thank you
so much." He leaves me and for a few moments I am all alone
in the room, no one watching me. A smile creeps onto my
face as I think of how perfectly this storm has all come
together — albeit faster than I had thought.

I have one lose end to tie up, and I text her to come and
fetch me.

They call me to see Gwen. I take a walk down the
corridor and into the room where my wife just killed herself.
It's clean now, no sign that Julia was ever here. The white
walls and floor wiped clean, and the bedsheets crisp and
fresh. The smell of Lysol and fear fill my nostrils as I take a
breath, and walk towards Gwen. The nurse who was
watching her steps out, and allows us a *family* moment.

"Oh Gwen, you're such a good girl. You finally grew a
back bone." She opens her mouth to scream, but I put my
bloodied hand over it before she can. I get so close, I can see
her pupils as they dilate. "You're going to be so happy here,
everyone will love you. The medicine will keep that little
devil from slipping out again. If you misbehave, the doctor
will sort you out. You remember him, don't you?" Bradley
stands in the doorway. Her eyes go wide and start to tear
with salty tears. She shakes her head under my hand. I can
feel her body tremble. I will never understand why she is
mad, the short-circuit in her brain. Maybe I took all the good
genes in the womb, because Gwen is mad, David was stupid
— and I'm perfect.
　　***

"Jack." Sarah shoots up out of the chair in the waiting
room, then realizes where we are and contains herself. The

switch goes, and she's the demure, professional office assistant without a single emotion showing on her porcelain face.

"Thank you for coming. I had no one to call," I say, putting on a little show for the staff.

"It's no problem, Mr Boyd. Let's get you home." I like professional Sarah. She's fuckable, intelligent and almost useful. Her high heels click-clack on the floor as we leave down the long hallway, and out the front doors. Once we exit the front door into the dead of night, mist hides the shadows and dark corners, and Sarah takes my hand in hers. My heart flutters with a momentary 'what-if' before we walk along the damp sidewalk to her car. Her perfume is soft and sophisticated, the delicate scent matches her carefully chosen outfit.

I don't let her drive, I never would — women are terrible drivers and I am fine to drive. In fact, I feel better than I have since I found out my brother had screwed my treacherous wife, and told her about Bradley. She thought by being perfect, I wouldn't notice, but I notice everything. She thought she could fix me by changing herself. *Stupid woman.* I notice things, that's why I am alive and they're all dead. The way I noticed how much he liked *my* Sarah. I never liked sharing my toys with my siblings. And when I saw the cracks in Gwen, when she started to fall apart, I noticed it and he didn't. I wonder if he ever knew that she saw him with Julia, that she came to me and told me — babbling like a nutcase. That night broke her, why did no one love her and everyone loved Julia.

Sarah puts her hand on my thigh, right where Julia's blood stains the fabric of my pants. I should feel guilt, sadness — anything. Instead, my dick gets hard when I see her red manicure, and I imagine those nails biting into my skin when I fuck her. The atmosphere changes and professional Sarah dissolves into Sarah the slut. I can't drive fast enough.

Wheels squeal as we pull into my garage a little too fast. I make sure the door is closed so no one can see us before we go into the house. *Appearance is everything.*

Sarah walks into my house like she was made to be here, and pours me a rum from the wet bar. *Perfect wife material.* She strips the blood stained clothes from my body as I sip on our victory, both my problems taken care of, and I didn't need to do a thing. Who knew it was so easy to drive a person crazy, so simple to break their mind like a toothpick. Sarah's nails drag up my thighs after she discards of my pants. On her knees, those perfectly painted red lips parted just slightly, looking up at me through her lashes. Julia's blood is still on my skin, marking me as hers.

I fist my cock, it's already hard at the thought of the freedom that finally awaits. She kneels below me, eagerly looking up, getting more excited as my breaths get noisier.

"Fuck," I grunt.

"Yes," She murmurs.

"I'm going to come," I moan.

Sarah opens her mouth, smiling, tongue out. *I'm going to miss her greedy little mouth.*

"Fuuuck!" I growl as I start to erupt into her waiting mouth. Painting her pretty face in my cum, I stand over her and imagine how this would have gone had she not been so eager to please my brother too. I rub my cock, milking it until the last drop. When I'm done she has my cum on her breast, face and tongue. She is like a Jackson Pollock painting. Keeping eye contact, she swallows, then wipes her chin with her finger and sucks it clean.

"Fuck, you're so sexy," I gasp.

"You're sexy," she says a shy smile on those ruined red lips. "That was the hottest thing I've seen in my life. Death and destruction suits you," She says, looking at me adoringly, like she admires the fact that I just wiped out my entire family in a single evening. Looking into her sultry eyes, my cock is already getting hard.

"Let's go take a bath, tie you up and get dirty all over again," I say, holding my hand out to help her up off the floor. Her cheeks blush and she looks down, biting that plump bottom lip. Ushering her up the stairs to the master bathroom, I whisper to her, "You look so pretty with my cum on your face, baby." She giggles and acts shy, I know better. Sarah only pretends to be shy. "My pretty little fuck doll, what am I going to do with you? You know all my secrets."

"You can do anything you want with me — Sir," She teases. "That's why you *love* me, isn't it?" I don't love her, but I certainly love fucking her.

"I'm going to shower and get Julia off of me. I expect you to be ass up on the bed waiting for me." I smack her perfect, firm ass and close the bathroom door between us. Sarah is a loose end, and as much as I enjoy her company, she has to go.
***

I hold her hips, and she grips the edge of the bed as best she can with her bound hands, while I fuck her with long steady strokes. Drawing my cock nearly all the way out before sliding back in deep. Steady, hypnotizing strokes.

"Feel my cock, baby. Feel how hard it is," I grunt in her ear, my body bent over hers, our sweat mixing. "Feel every vein bulging for you."

"Fuck," She sighs out as her orgasm grips her like my hand on her throat. Once she comes, I start to fuck her with more urgency.

I can feel my orgasm building, ready to crash on me soon.

"Fuck," I say without meaning to. Sarah is struggling to breathe, riding the end of her own wave and fighting the way my big hand is throttling her delicate neck. "Fuck, baby," I hiss, pulling out of her. Using my other hand I rub my cock fast.

"Yessss," I grind out, loudly, the veins in my neck bulging. I groan, and spurt my cum all over the bed sheets.

She didn't moan. She just went limp, lifeless, and collapsed forwards, sliding off the bed. Her head hitting the hardwood floor, her neck making a cracking sound as it jammed sideways. Her own body weight snapping it.

Well, that was convenient. I really didn't want to have to drown her in the bath full of bleach. I guess I can just clean her up now. Wouldn't want evidence or anything ruining my perfect plans.

I tie a bow around her with my tie and snap a picture of her, then send it off to Bradley with a caption.

Happy Valentines, my love. I got you the perfect gift.

ABOUT ASHLEIGH GIANNOCCARO

Ashleigh lives in sunny South Africa with her husband, children and pet meerkat Porky. She writes dark and twisted romance that will have you swooning over the villain in no time. When she's not writing she can be found traveling the country or with her nose in a book traveling to magical places no one has been.

Join Ashleigh's Facebook Reader Group!

ALSO BY ASHLEIGH GIANNOCCARO

Cirque Act 1

"If no one loves the clown.

Then I will make you no one."

Cut & Blow Book 1

"There's only one place to shampoo

your dirty mob money."

Written In Flames

"Broken people shouldn't play with matches"

FIRST CHAPTER TEASERS

FIGHT ME, DADDY

BY ZOE BLAKE

How deep does a grave have to be?

Wasn't there something about animals?

Chloe gripped the small heart charm which hung about her neck, taking solace as the metal warmed beneath her hand. The blue-white beam of her flashlight bounced off dark tree trunks and the thick bed of wet leaves and twigs which covered the ground.

Would the rain make digging easier or harder she wondered?

The sound of crunching gravel alerted her to a car traveling up the long driveway even before she saw the headlights. Turning off her flashlight, she ran back towards the cabin, tripping over a half-buried log in her haste. Throwing open the rough wooden gate that separated the forest from the clearing, she raced across the yard, ignoring the ice cold water that seeped into her sneakers as her feet sank into the rain-soaked grass. Cringing at the loud squeak the back screen door made as she carefully opened it, Chloe crouched low as she crossed the study into the kitchen. Keeping her head down, she reached up and turned off the small lamp she always kept lit on her kitchen table. Without the soft warm glow, the cabin felt cold and still.

Chloe held her breath, straining to hear the sound of any movement outside. A car door. The sound of an engine turning off. If there was a god, the sound of gravel as the car turned around and left.

Silence.

The anxiety of not knowing was too much. Chloe crawled across the linoleum, around the kitchen island. She paused and listened.

Still nothing.

Trying to calm her pounding heart, she crept closer to the front door. Her knees ached from crawling on the hard floor. Her damp jeans chafed and clung to her hips with every movement. She could feel mud squishing between her toes inside her sneakers. All she wanted was to take a hot shower and forget this night ever happened. But that wasn't possible…she could never wash away the horror of this night.

Grimacing as small pebbles, tracked inside from the driveway, cut into the palms of her hands, Chloe slowly crept into the mud room. The front door was straight ahead. It had an open window pane, so she kept low and to the shadows. Just beyond was the small porch and the gravel drive. Leaning against the wall to the right of the door, Chloe tilted her head and listened.

More silence.

Her heartbeat finally slowed.

It must have been a neighbor driving by.

"Chloe. Open the door."

Throwing her hand over her mouth to stifle a scream, Chloe scurried farther back along the wall, staring at the closed door with wild eyes.

There was another long, excruciating pause.

Then.

"I know you are in there. I need you to open the door."

The dark command of his voice almost had her obeying. How did he know her name? Who was he? The police? She would have welcomed the police. An hour ago. But not now. Now it was too late. Maybe he was a friend of *his*. Just another reason why she couldn't open the door. The cabin was dark. The doors locked. Her car was parked in the garage with the door closed. There was no real way for him to know she was inside. Maybe if she stayed quiet, he would give up and leave?

"Baby, I'm losing my patience. Trust me. You don't want that."

The deep tone of the stranger's voice was getting harsher. Did she dare continue to defy him?

She moved her hand over the low shelf that ran along the wall at her back, encountering bug candles, rubber boots, and fishing tackle. Nothing that could be used as a weapon. There were her late uncle's hunting rifles in the gun cabinet in the living room, but she would have to crawl back through the kitchen. The cabin was dark, but there was no way he would not see the outline of her movements through the front door window now that he was standing just on the other side. The door wasn't even secured with a deadbolt, just a simple key lock. She lived in a cabin in the woods in the middle of nowhere in upstate Michigan where all the neighbors knew one another. There wasn't a need for extraneous locks and deadbolts.

"I'm giving you one last chance to open this door, babygirl," the stranger growled.

Chloe knew the old door with its old lock would not hold. She needed to make a decision.

The door handle rattled violently.

She was out of time.

Rising up, Chloe bolted back through the kitchen.

The sickening sound of splintering wood and shattering glass reverberated throughout the cabin.

Chloe's wet soles skidded along the floor as she sharply turned right down the narrow hallway to the living room. The gun cabinet was just over the threshold. Her trembling hand closed over the brass handle. The guns weren't loaded, but hopefully the stranger wouldn't get close enough to notice. Wrenching the handle upwards, Chloe threw open the cabinet door and blindly reached in, feeling for the cold barrel of the rifle she knew was there.

A hand closed over her shoulder, spinning her about and slamming her against the wall. She had no chance to even scream. That same hand wrapped around her throat, the long fingers easily encircling the slender column till her jaw was pushed upwards, her head crushed painfully against the wall.

The sharp angles of the stranger's face came into focus. His angry, lowered brow. Dark, unreadable eyes.

His full lips lifted in a sneer. "I warned you, baby."

Chloe tried to rise up on her toes to ease the pressure on her throat. Desperately, she clawed at the man's t-shirt. A garbled scream escaped her lips.

"Shhh…all that will do is piss me off more than I already am, and we don't want that do we?" He'd leaned in close to whisper the ominous threat, his lips skimming along her jaw. The scrape of his stubble rubbed against the soft skin of her cheek.

She tried to shake her head no, but his grip on her throat would not allow it.

He spread his legs wide before leaning his hips forward, pressing into her body. He was a large beast of a man. Both his size and voice were frightening…intimidating.

He ran the back of his knuckles down her cheek. "Now, you are going to be a good girl and obey me."

Chloe tried to convey her willingness with her eyes.

He seemed to understand because he released his grip on her throat, but he shifted his hips as if to remind her he still held a portion of her body prisoner. As if she needed reminding.

With a warning look in her direction, he flicked on the switch by her shoulder.

Chloe blinked as the room flooded with light. The moment her eyes adjusted, she caught her first real look at the stranger who had forced his way into her cabin. If he had not been holding her against the wall, her knees would have given out in sheer fright. Jesus Christ! The man looked like the type of prison thug you only saw in the movies...or mug shots on the news. Impossibly tall, his chest and arms were thick with muscle. He had a neck tattoo. *A goddamn neck tattoo.* Piercing blue eyes watched her with amusement.

"You like what you see, babygirl?"

Oh god, thought Chloe. She had survived one horror this night only to be raped and murdered by this man.

Maybe it was what she deserved.

He ran a finger over her collarbone and then traced the V-neck edge of her pink t-shirt.

Chloe bit her lip to keep from crying out. Her fists were clenched so hard, her palms hurt from where her fingernails bit into them.

Still he taunted her. His finger slowly ran up and down the edge of her neckline, till it dipped into the low vee. Hooking his finger into the flimsy, damp fabric, he pulled it towards him.

Chloe cried out in alarm and started to defensively raise her arms.

"Don't," he ordered.

She had no choice but to lower her limbs helplessly to her sides.

Her t-shirt gaped open, exposing her to his intense gaze.

Chloe closed her eyes in mortification. The generous top curves of her breasts encased in delicate white lace were clearly on display. Embroidered onto the bra, right in the center, nestled in her cleavage was a small pink design.

The stranger raised one dark eyebrow. "Hello Kitty?"

Chloe slowly nodded her head yes.

"Later I'm going to want a closer look at this cute bra, but for now, we have some business to attend to."

A warm tear escaped the corner of her eye. *Later?* Her stomach twisted.

Her cabin was isolated and hard to reach during the day, let alone during a torrential storm in the middle of the night. Even if she were willing to call the police, they would never reach her in time. It would take the small force of Glennie at least an hour to respond to her call for help. She shuddered to think what this dangerous man could do to her in the span of an hour.

"Please," she choked out. "The stones are in my office. In the safe."

"Stones?"

"The diamonds. Just take them."

The man chuckled. The sinister sound was devoid of any mirth.

"I don't give a fuck about any diamonds."

"Then what do you want?"

The moment the question left her lips, she knew it was a mistake.

The man leaned in with his hips. The hard ridge of his arousal pressed against her stomach.

Chloe whimpered as she shifted her body to the side, desperately trying to break his hold.

What kind of man turned down diamonds? A crazy fuck, that's who.

Chloe didn't trust anyone who claimed to not be interested in money. Money was cold, unfeeling. Straightforward. Every horrible moment in her fucked up, twisted life could be traced back to someone else's need for money. At least it made things uncomplicated. There was no wondering why or any deep self-reflection or even a need for that elusive idea of closure or meaning. She knew why…money.

There was only one other thing besides money that could influence a person's actions…sex.

She could feel the ominous power of his *intention* as he used his body to cage her own.

She would not give in without a fight. Clenching her small hand into a fist, she lashed out. The fifteen carat, vintage amethyst ring she always wore caught him on the cheekbone. A droplet of blood trickled from the scratch caused by one of the diamond accents.

He raised two fingertips to swipe at the blood. Keeping his eyes trained on hers, his tongue flicked out to taste the crimson drop.

Watching him, she could almost taste the metallic tang on her own tongue.

"I was hoping you would fight me. It will make this all so much easier."

Her scream was lost in the deep, dark woods.

One Click Fight Me, Daddy here!

BRANDED CAPTIVE

BY ADDISON CAIN

"Accept my seed, Omega."

The breath wafting over her cheek was rancid, but it was the last thing Wren might take stock of when that *thing* was cracking her pelvis in half. She had done as she'd been instructed. Remained docile when the man had yanked her legs embarrassingly wide over his thighs. She had even ignored the thick thatch of coarse salt and pepper hair on his chest scratching her back when he hoisted her up.

He'd growled as her mother told her he would, and torn through her barrier with one impatient yank of her hips. Unable to scream, Wren had only arched her spine, head thrown back on his shoulder. The Alpha, either oblivious or uncaring for her comfort, grasped her hips, bobbing her up and down his veined cock three times. With the fourth rude shunt, he'd clawed at her softer places and driven her down until her ass cheeks slapped against his lap. Immediately something ballooned inside her aching guts. It pressed her bladder to the point Wren was certain she'd dribbled more than a little piss on her buyer, continuing to expand until squished bowels, organs, and jangled nerves all screamed for relief.

"Damn you, Omega. Take my seed!"

Take what where? She didn't understand what she was supposed to do now.

At her back, the stranger panted, shifting beneath her as if he too were extremely uncomfortable. When she failed to perform, his irritation quickly translated into anger. The stink invaded Wren's nostrils, it made her skin buzz.

Angry Alphas killed.

Angry Alphas must always be appeased.

Staring forward across the dimly lit, yet finely appointed space, Wren inhaled and exhaled on the count of three. There was nothing to be done about the stinging stretch where her legs were hooked over the man's spread thighs. He had not offered to take her to a bed or even asked to see her build a nest. No, the couch in his fine house's receiving room had suited his purpose well enough.

Examine and test the stock.

Fuck the virgin with her father on the other side of the cracked door.

The man who'd brought her to sell listening to this. To the Alpha's strained breaths, to his grunts and wheezing.

Her father was listening to her failure.

Wren forced herself to look down. She had not seen the Alpha's cock before he'd shunted it unexpectedly into her, or even had a good look at the male. Her eyes had been downcast when they arrived, lest her father strike her for insolence. She had disrobed for inspection. She had moved as commanded and not resisted when the Alpha yanked her to the nearest seat.

And her father had exited the room to listen so he might claim full payment for what transpired.

Payment for... *this*. Wren stared where only the root of an

Alpha cock was visible stretching her labia beyond imagining. There was a little blood, far less than she'd anticipated considering the sting. The red spread with their fluids, matting the hair that peppered his swollen ball sack.

The knot in her belly gave an angry pulse, expanding again in a bid to ruin her completely. Gnashing his teeth, the Alpha almost whined against her neck, his balls thundering in twitching pulses. They too expanded, the skin under all that coarse hair growing shiny and white from the stretch.

"Fucking Omega…" A meaty hand left her hip, landing on her belly as if that might force her even further down his meat. But there was nowhere else to go. She was tied to him by that pulsating knot spreading agony in her guts. From the way he fought to speak, how his breath hitched in a whine with each breath, the Alpha was in as much pain as she. "You have one purpose. Milk my fucking cock!"

If that knot kept banging against her pubic bone, she was going to be sick all over his rug. Stalled, unsure what it was he wanted from her, Wren thought the wisest course was to remain still and wait.

It was the wrong choice.

"Your freak daughter is failing to comply!" The snarled shout was directed to the cracked door.

The meek response was never the tone Wren's father took with her. "Have you… umm… stimulated her, sir?"

Wren's new owner turned his head, yelling so sharply the girl flinched. "Of course I have! She belligerently refuses to bring me to orgasm. My fucking knot is full. Gah—" Slick with sweat, the Alpha squeezed her tighter, caught in a waving cramp of his own. "I'll have your goddamn head for this, Carson!"

"Wren, honey." Through the cracked door, her father sing-songed, "Relax and take his seed. Show this illustrious Alpha you wish to serve as his mate."

I wanted to sign that I didn't understand, to reach out for the man who'd brought me here to sell me. But he could not see me.

My potential mate roared, "SEND IN HELENA!"

Another door in the chilly room opened, a woman in a vivid robe rushing forward. "How can I serve you, my Alpha?"

"Bend over the desk and wait for me!"

Wren watched the woman quickly strip, viewing another naked female body for the first time in her life. With no preamble, the pretty brunette bent at the waist, the globes of her ass presented, her cheek to the wood.

Beta female parts were on display.

Cruel fingers reached for Wren's stretched labia, the Alpha yanking at the sensitive flesh as he grunted and threw her forward with his weight. His ballooning testicles doubled in size, the man groaning with the worst sort of agony.

His pain was nothing to hers. The knot that was meant to tie them together in life was deformed by his tricks until it could be pulled free of her body. Wren was dumped on the floor, hand pressed between her trembling legs as she wailed.

From the corner of her eye, she watched the Alpha scythe his cock into the waiting female, wrecking her with the madness of his need to release. Unlike Wren, the Beta gave him immediate relief, the Alpha's cry earsplitting.

Bowed over, curled in on herself, Wren shut her eyes to it all.

When her father was called forward, even then she refused to rise to meet his gaze. Naked and shamed on the floor of a stranger's house, she sniffed, wishing she couldn't hear the terrible things that were said about her.

"Was she not trained?"

"My wife took great pains to explain what would be expected, sir. You have my humblest apologies that she failed, but if you are not going to take her as your new mate, you still owe for the tearing of her hymen. She will be harder to sell unintact."

Of course her father would try to weasel credits from this man...

The Alpha gave an incredulous laugh. "Your mute albino freak might be pretty to look at, but she is the worst fuck imaginable. If you think I'd expose that cunt to another Alpha in this city, you're wrong."

"You owe me one-thousand credits for her virginity!" Her father never once came to her defense, never offered her comfort, he only tried to squeeze what he could from a far richer man. "The contract was clear. No matter the outcome of the first mating, a fee will be paid!"

The sound of ice hitting the side of crystal, the pour of liquor. Far calmer, the Alpha took a long sip. "The contract," a smile in his voice, the Alpha purred, "is null and void if the merchandise is defective. You get nothing, Carson. She will be tagged and dumped in the Warrens and you will leave here grateful to be breathing."

No! Ignoring sore muscles and the screaming pain between her legs, Wren scampered to her father and wrapped her arm around his leg. Signing frantically, she begged him for mercy.

He looked down at his pale, violet-eyed child, deadpan as he said, "I should have had you euthanized at birth."

One click Branded Captive here!

THE MAIDEN

BY CELIA AARON

Sheer white fabric covers me from neck to toe. I keep my eyes on the dirt path ahead of me as I move through the dark, my thin shift a beacon in the night calling every sort of predator to me. I try not to shiver. Keeping my steps even becomes my world, my only focus. One step, then the next.

I can't think about the crackling branches, the footfalls through the crisp leaves, the low chant floating through the chilly air, or the women ahead or behind me. No. Only my own steps. Right, then left. The frozen earth beneath my bare feet. The momentum that carries me deeper and deeper into the woods.

Firelight casts a faint glow as we continue moving forward, each of us rushing toward the cage, desire in our hearts, and fervor in our souls. We want to be shackled, owned, moved only by the spirit of our God. And our God has anointed one on earth to embody His good will. The Prophet Leon Monroe.

The deep chant thrums through my veins as I approach the firelight, the orange glimmer flickering over my dirty feet and up to play against the soft fabric of my nightgown.

Though clothed, I am bare. I enter the circle of men, each one of them dressed in white pants and shirts—holy men, handpicked by the Prophet himself.

I follow the girl ahead of me until all of us form an inner circle, pressed between the fire and the men along the outside. It's a new circle of hell, promising an agonizing burn no matter which way I move.

A woman in all black walks along the line of women, handing each of us a small pitcher of water. My head bowed, I don't look her in the eye as she approaches. But I already know who she is—Rachel—first wife of the Prophet. Her limp gives her away. I take my pitcher, the weight of the cold water steadying the shake in my hands.

A strong voice silences the chanting. "We thank God for this bounty."

"Amen," the men chorus.

"We remember His commandment to 'Be fruitful and increase in number.' As a sign of our obedience to His will, we take these girls under our care, our protection. We also take them into our hearts, to cherish as if they were of our own blood."

"Amen."

His voice grows louder as he walks around the circle. "Just as Rebekah was called by the Lord to marry a son of Abraham, so have these girls been called to serve the godly men gathered here tonight."

A pair of heavy boots stops in front of me. A light touch under my chin pulls my gaze upward until I'm met by a pair of dark eyes. The Prophet peers into my soul.

"Do you remember the tale of Rebekah, Sister?"

"Yes, Prophet."

"I'm sure a child of God like you knows all the stories in the Bible." He smiles, his white teeth bleached like a skeleton's.

"Yes, Prophet."

"'The woman was very beautiful, a virgin; no man had ever slept with her. She went down to the spring, filled her jar and came up again.' And then what happened to Rebekah?"

"She was taken by Abraham's servant."

"That's correct." He leans closer, his gaze boring into mine.

A shiver courses through me. He glances down at my chest, a smirk twisting the side of his lips as he sees my hard nipples through the gauzy fabric.

He releases my chin and steps back, continuing his circuit as he speaks of Rebekah's destiny. I steal a look at the man standing opposite me. Blond hair, blue eyes, a placid expression—the Prophet's youngest son. Something akin to relief washes over me. Being Cloister Maiden to Noah Monroe wouldn't be so bad. He was rumored to be kind, gentle even. I let my gaze slide to the man standing at his left. Dark hair, even darker eyes, and a smirk like his father's on his lips as he stares at me—Adam Monroe. I drop my gaze and silently pity the Maiden to my right.

"We will keep you safe. Away from the monsters of this world who would seek to use you, to destroy the innocent perfection that each one of you possess. Remember the story of Dinah: 'When Shechem, son of Hamor the Hivite, the ruler of that area, saw her, he took her and raped her.' And so it is with any man who is not within this circle. They would take you, hurt you, and cast you aside once they've spoiled your body and heart. Only in the Cloister can you lead peaceful lives without fear."

I wonder if Georgia heard the same speech. She must have. How long did they let her live after this ritual? The thought churns inside me, surprisingly strong, and hate begins to override my meek persona. Breaking character for a split second, I glance back up at Adam Monroe. Had he been the one to slit her throat? Had his large hands done untold violence to Georgia while she was still alive?

He scowls at the shivering Maiden standing in front of him, then snaps his gaze to meet mine. His eyes round the slightest bit, and I drop my focus back to the dirt, then close my eyes. I shouldn't have done that. I silently berate myself as Leon—*no, he's the Prophet*—as *the Prophet* continues his lesson on the safety of the Cloister. I let my disguise fall back into place. I am a devout follower of the Prophet and eager Cloister Maiden. The hum of my thoughts grows louder, and I realize the Prophet has stopped talking.

I open my eyes and peek at the Maiden to my left. She's lifted her pitcher, her eyes still downcast. I do the same.

"The water signifies an offering from Maiden to her Protector. A righteous man—one who will teach her and lead her in the light of the Lord our God. The Protector is sanctified by God, and his decisions will always be made in the best interest of the Maiden under his protection. Just as God instructed in Genesis, the man is leader, the woman his helpmate. And so it will be here. The Protector—with God in his heart—shall lead his Maiden and show her the ways of true believers."

"Amen." The men's voices seem to have grown louder, hungrier.

"Now, Maidens, offer yourselves as vessels made to carry the knowledge and light of our Lord, to your Protector."

With shaking arms, I hold out my pitcher. A brief brush of fingers against mine, and the weight lifts. After a few moments, the drained pitchers fly over our heads and crash into the fire at our backs. A primal roar rips from the men—wolves with appetites whetted for blood.

"Protectors, lead your gentle lambs back to the Cloister where we will welcome them into the fold."

A hand appears, the wide palm up. I take a deep breath and remind myself that Noah is a good draw. Slipping my hand into his, I lift my eyes to find the entirely wrong man attached. Noah leads a different woman away from the bonfire.

Adam's smirk darkens as he grips my hand too tight. "Shall we, little lamb?"

One Click The Maiden here!

WHITE PAWN

BY SJ COLE

"So, no suicidal thoughts, no ideations?"

Dr. Hallman sits at his mahogany desk behind mounds of patient files. The deep lines set around his mouth reminds me of a marionette and I wonder what he'd look like with those little strings tied to his arms, someone forcing his arms and legs up and down. Inhaling, he folds his hands as his eyes set on me. "Yes? No?"

I smile. "No."

"So the medication has been helpful?"

"I think so, I mean, I feel better, but I haven't noticed any weird side effects or anything like that." The air conditioner kicks on, the tick-tick-tick of it causing me to shift uncomfortably in my seat. I want to get up and slam my fist over it.

"That's good." He makes a note in my file as he scratches over his salt-and-pepper beard. Depression. It's a pain in the ass. You have one moment where you think life's not worth living and slit your wrists, and then you're whisked away to a hospital and put on fucking suicide watch. I've been here for three weeks and I am ready to get on with my life. I bounce my leg anxiously, watching as the light blue gown slides up my thigh. Dr. Hallman glances up from his paperwork. "The orderlies said you've been reading."

"Yes."

"What?"

Why does it matter what I've been reading? If I say Stephen King's *Doctor Sleep* are they going to think I'm a crazed murder who wants to off an entire family? "Um, Justin Wild, ever heard of him?"

"No." He shakes his head. "Any good?

"Yes, very good actually. Dark romance, I think is what the genre is called."

He doesn't respond, just keeps jotting something down on his little pad. And then, he looks up and smiles. His thin lips curl around coffee-stained teeth. "Ms. Dawson—"

I cringe. "Marisa. Please call me Marisa." I can't stand hearing that last name because it was John's. And John is the reason I'm here in the first place.

Dr. Hallman's lips twitch ever so slightly as he taps his heavy, silver pen over the desk. "Marisa, nervous break-downs aren't that uncommon, especially in people who have dealt with what you've dealt with."

I close my eyes and sweat slowly pricks its way under-neath the collar of my hospital gown. I feel the thin material begin to stick to my back and I grip the armrests of the chair, my fingers squeaking over the leather. All I can see is John, his lifeless body slumped over, blood splattered all over the $7,000 French oil painting we bought at auction on our honeymoon. He blew his brains out because he couldn't be with *her*—with his whore. His *blonde* fucking whore.

"Marisa…"

I open my eyes and stare through Dr. Hallman, my vision swimming behind tears. "I'm sorry," I whisper, "you were saying?"

"You've been through a lot. The affair, all the unraveling of John's lies about what he did, who he was, and then, his death." He closes the file folder in front of him, pushes the stack of files to the side, and leans across the desk. "But you are going to be okay." I nod even though I don't believe him. I just want out of here. I just want to go home. Back to whatever life it is I have left.

"Just make sure you keep up with your medications and appointments, and you call us if you ever need us. Okay?" He stands from behind his desk, the wheels to his chair squeaking as it rolls back. I take that as my cue to leave.

"When do I get to go home?" I ask.

"I'm putting in orders to have you discharged this afternoon. Do you have someone to come pick you up?" I nod as I stand from my chair and head to the door. I don't need to tell him I'll call an Uber, that I don't have any friends left after John had isolated me from everyone. My pathetic life is no longer of his business. "Good. And Marisa," he says, "try to take it easy on yourself, okay?"

"Okay," I whisper as I place my hand on the door and walk out into the overly-sterilized hallway of the psychiatric ward. I go to my room and pack my few belongings: a toothbrush and the three copies of Justin's books one of the orderlies gave me. The have the little barcode from the hospital library, but, I'm not returning them. My tears have seeped into the crème paper. The words within each chapter stole the little remnants left of my heart, so, I'm keeping them.

The nurse comes by at noon and I receive my discharge papers. There's no fanfare, no farewell party. I just sign out and walk through the front doors. Alone. The white Camry with the Uber sticker is waiting for me in the roundabout. I place my bag in the trunk and give the driver, Adam from Georgia, the address to my old house.

The rural Tennessee landscape whirls past the window.

Pines and cow pastures lined by wire fencing, but it's all a blur because I'm in a daze, dreaming about Meredith and Lucas—the characters in Justin's book. I have three chapters to go until I finish the last in the series, and I'm on pins and needles. Everything is so up in the air at this point. She's been kidnapped and Lucas is on a killing rampage trying to find her. I worry how this will end, but I believe Justin will have them together. I can *feel* it. It's as though—I don't know, as though I know him. Like reading his words, well, like I'm reading my *own* words. I can feel what's going to happen. I can finish the next sentence.

The cab rolls to a slow stop in front of my house, the large white antebellum home with the beautiful navy door and shutters. I loved this house when John first showed it to me. Everything about it was perfect. It had four bedrooms and three baths, a formal living room and dining room. A fireplace in the master bedroom and rich cherry bookshelves in the study. My stomach knots and slips when my gaze lands on the red "Under Contract" addition to the For Sale sign. We put it on the market after I found out about his affair. His affair with that slutty blonde that worked as his paralegal. The sign's still crooked, I'd hoped someone would have corrected that by now. It's just another fucking reminder. The sight of your dear husband's head blown to bits is quite the horror, and I ran out screaming. I made it as far as the sign before my head began to spin and I passed out, hitting the sign and landing on the lawn.

I tip the driver, grab my bag from the trunk, and stand at the end of the sidewalk, staring at the huge blooms on the Magnolia tree in the front yard. I hate this house now. I hate everything about it, everything about my life. I don't want to go inside, so I don't. I drop my bag at the end of the sidewalk and sit on it, opening my book and losing myself in a world I wish I belonged to.

It only takes me half an hour to get through the last 50 pages. My heart thumps and jumps, my lungs fight to pull in my next breath as I turn the page and then...I gasp, shaking my head angrily. "No. No. No!" I mumble, my throat growing tight as I stare down at the blurry words. Tears fall, staining the page. The words "The End".

Meredith shoots herself because she doesn't want to live without Lucas. That's it. Puts a gun to her head and *pow*. And Lucas is left heartbroken and alone, never to love a woman again. Where is the happily ever after? My face heats. My nostrils flare. "No!" I turn and chuck the book at the crooked For Sale sign, the chain to the "Sold" addition creaking as the sign sways in the breeze. I stare at the book sprawled out on the green lawn, it's pages bent and spine split, and then, guilt consumes me. I quickly stand and jog across the yard to pick it up and dust it off. It's not what I wanted, but, after all, it's not my story.

It's not my story. It's Justin's.

It's Justin's.

_____

One Year Later

It's half past midnight, the white light from the city spills in through the living room window and pours across the blonde hardwood floors. Sighing, I get to my feet and stretch. My muscles ache, my neck is stiff from shuffling around moving boxes. I've spent all day unpacking, putting everything in its place in my new home on Water Street. The insurance money came in a month ago, twelve months to the day that John killed himself. Evidently, he'd renewed the policy two years to the date before he died, ticking up from a one-million-dollar policy to two. The insurance company squabbled about it for months, even though the clause says two years before a suicide and the money goes to the spouse. I guess they want it to be two years and a day. Idiots. And It couldn't have come in a day sooner. My bank account was slim, having lived off mine and John's savings for the past year. I never worked when I was with John. He didn't want me to, and besides, being one of the best defense attorneys on the east coast, it's not like we needed extra money. I just needed to get out of that house, that town. Everything reminded me of him. Everywhere I went, I pictured him and his whore. I needed a fresh start. And here it is. Manhattan. DUMBO. A padded bank account and the opportunity to start writing books with the endings they deserve.

I curl up on my sofa with a half empty bottle of wine, a blanket, and my well-read copy of *Reality* open on my lap. I swore I'd never read those books again because they gutted me, but, after a few weeks, when I couldn't stop thinking about Lucas…I found myself reading them again and again. And each time, the ending hurt just as much as it did the first time. I run my finger beneath the printed words, reading them aloud: *And in the end, that is all there is. Perception. Be it deep or shallow, love is nothing more than a figment of our imaginations. And, oh what a shame it was when I discovered that it all, every miniscule piece of it, was meaningless. All of it except for Meredith because for a moment in time, she was mine. She was my story and I was hers…*

I draw in a breath. A deep breath. Those words. *His* words —unmatched by any other author. I close the hardback book, flipping it over to look at his picture, and I find myself swooning. Justin Wild's face is as beautiful as his words. I skim over the author bio, which, by now, I know by heart: Justin Wild is the self-published author of the worldwide bestselling books *Delusion, Illusion,* and *Reality.* He began writing as a graduate student studying Forensic Psychology at Emory University, publishing his trilogy a week after he graduated with honors. He lives in Manhattan, New York with his beloved Great Dane, Cobain (named after the world's greatest musician: Kurt Cobain. God rest his soul).

Closing the paperback, I sink into the couch cushions. I think this makes the 77th time I've read this book. I have the lines memorized. A person capable of writing such an epic story—there must be something immeasurably deep to him. And there is...I've read every interview he's done with blogs and any article he's had a hand in. I follow him on every social media platform that exists, and thanks to his posts, I feel like I *know* Justin. I know where he shops, what his favorite foods are. I know what TV shows he watches, which actresses he fantasizes about. He likes brunettes and I can't blame him. Blondes are trashy sluts. Sometimes he posts about his dreams. . .his day to day thoughts. The selfies. The livefeeds. I know that if I ever run into him, he'll realize we belong together. Fate. Sometimes I am certain it was fate that had John take his own life. If he'd never killed himself, I'd have never ended up in that psych ward and I'd never have found Justin's beautiful books. Never known such a perfect soul was out there, wandering, waiting, searching...

I set the book on the coffee table and trudge into my bedroom, skirting around moving boxes. I lie down, close my eyes, but I can't find sleep. The noise of the New York City traffic is louder than the silence of the country. The windows in my apartment are old and thin, and every sound seems to amplify when it passes through glass, but I do love my apartment. DUMBO is a wonderful little neighborhood, expensive, but so worth it. I can see why Justin chose to live here. On Water Street.

Don't worry, that had little to do with why *I* moved onto Water Street—it's just such a nice area, with an amazing view of the city. And I'm certain, one day, fate will have me run into him.

One Click White Pawn here!

STEALING BEAUTY

BY JULIA SYKES

Pale green eyes sliced into my chest, their cutting gaze keener than I remembered. They practically glowed as he glowered at me from across the church: a panther deciding whether his prey was worth bothering with the hunt. His full lips curled in a sneer, those beautiful, terrifying eyes scanning my body.

Whatever he saw in me, he decided I wasn't worth his time. He blinked and looked away, his attention turning back to the stunning blonde draped on his arm.

I sucked in a gasp, remembering how to breathe. My fingers trembled at my sides as a hit of adrenaline surged through my system.

I'd known Adrián would be here. I'd told myself I was ready to face him. I'd told myself that I'd be able to mask my ire and put on the pretty, pleasant smile that was expected of me.

But I hadn't been prepared for the hatred in his burning stare. Ten long years had passed since I'd last looked into those hypnotic green eyes. Once, they'd shined with devotion when he looked at me.

Now, it seemed he loathed me as much as I despised him.

I collected my wits, clenching my fists at my sides to still my shaking fingers. My perfectly manicured nails bit into my palms, but I welcomed the little flare of pain. It helped ground me. Pain reminded me of my role, my duties.

I'd receive a lot more of it if I didn't play my part perfectly: devoted wife to Hugo Sánchez, the second most powerful man in Bogotá.

The most powerful man, Vicente Rodríguez, was the reason I was here, participating in this farce.

A visible shiver raced through the young woman—barely more than a girl—who stood at the altar. Camila Gómez had the misfortune of catching Vicente's eye a year ago. The eighteen-year-old had gotten pregnant, giving him a son. He'd decided to force her into this marriage to ensure the boy's legitimacy. A secondary heir to his cocaine empire, in case something were to happen to Adrián.

Adrián Rodríguez. I could hardly believe the boy I'd loved all those years ago had turned into the hard, frightening man who'd taken his place in the church pew behind me. I couldn't see him, but I could feel his cruel glare on my back. It made my skin pebble with a prey's awareness, my body instinctively sensing the threat.

For the last decade, he'd been in America, consolidating the power of his father's cartel in California. I'd never expected to see him again, but Vicente's wedding to poor Camila had brought the prodigal son home to Colombia.

The girl's petite frame appeared smaller than ever as she shrank in Vicente's shadow. He'd waited long enough for her slender body to return to its youthful perfection after she'd given birth—no doubt, she was kept on a careful regimen to ensure her beauty for this day.

I was far too familiar with the practice: the restricted diet and proscribed exercise to keep my natural curves just the right size to please my husband. Mercifully, Hugo stood at Vicente's side rather than mine. As Vicente's lapdog, Hugo was a natural choice to play the part of best man at this sham wedding.

My husband's beady black eyes fixed on me, and his thin lips curved into a malicious smile. An involuntary shudder wracked my body. He'd looked at me with the exact same expression ten years ago, when I'd been the one in the pretty white dress, forced to the altar against my will. I was only sixteen at the time, but Hugo hadn't minded being wedded to a child. He'd waited too long for his turn with me to care.

And as my guardian, Vicente had given me away to his best friend, gifting me to him in exchange for his years of loyalty.

I could hardly bear to look at either of the disgusting, lecherous men. Somehow, I lifted my chin and straightened my spine. I couldn't allow anyone in the church to sense that my fear-drenched memories of my wedding night were playing through my mind.

Hugo delighted in my fear, but he also expected me to maintain the façade of perfect, loving wife when we were in public. He might be short and stocky, but his rounded belly didn't diminish his strength. His thinning black hair and ruddy cheeks were showing the signs of his age, but the years hadn't caused him to grow frail. He was as brutal as he'd been on the day I'd met him, when I was fourteen years old.

I plastered on a beatific smile, meeting my husband's gaze. To any casual observer, I'd appear to be staring at him with love and devotion, remembering the false joy of our own wedding day.

Camila's palpable terror made the dark memories I kept locked at the back of my mind push to the forefront. I shoved them away before I gagged. A metallic tang coated my tongue, and I realized I'd bitten the inside of my cheek.

The ceremony passed by in a blur. I drew in deep breaths to suppress my rising nausea. When the priest pronounced Vicente and Camila husband and wife, I managed a wide smile. My eyes watered with empathy for the girl, but I'd be able to pass it off as tears of joy.

I followed the stream of guests as we exited the white and gold opulence of the basilica, stepping out into the heavy dusk heat. Hugo waited by the black limo outside the church, gesturing that I should get in the car. Vicente and Camila were already in their vintage Rolls-Royce, which would take them to the reception space: an imposing, historic *castillo* located outside Bogotá.

I smiled at my husband and took his hand, allowing him to help me slide into the back seat. He settled in beside me, pressing his doughy body close to mine. The sickening scent of his amber cologne mingling with his sweat washed over me. I'd become accustomed to it over the years, but today, the overpowering reek made me want to retch.

Seconds later, my nausea intensified. My gut lurched as Adrián got into the limo, his stunning blonde date sliding into place at his side. Her dark eyebrows didn't match her platinum locks, but the obvious dye job didn't diminish her beauty.

I couldn't focus on her, though. My eyes locked on Adrián's burning green stare.

My breath caught, and my pretty smile melted.

Hugo's meaty hand rested on my thigh, high enough to be indecent in front of strangers.

But Adrián wasn't a stranger. He was a ghost from my past. A horrifying apparition that appeared all too corporeal. His massive body filled the space, his bulk obvious even beneath his sharply-tailored black suit.

I could feel Hugo's hot breath on my face before he

pressed a wet, stomach-turning kiss against my cheek. "Are you all right, *cariña?*"

Adrián's nostrils flared, his full lips thinning. His square jaw hardened to granite, and his high cheekbones appeared sharper than ever.

For a moment, the world spun around me, the sickly-sweet stench of my husband powerful enough to make me lightheaded.

Hugo's fingers dug into my thigh, a clear warning to behave myself.

The flare of pain helped me focus. I tore my eyes from Adrián's, staring out the window instead.

"I'm fine," I managed.

I couldn't look at my husband. I could barely draw breath when he was so close, and Adrián's hatred pressing against me like a tangible force didn't help me breathe easier.

I tried to focus on the glittering lights as the city lit up around us, the historic sites of *La Candelaria* district beginning to glow against the falling darkness. The limo's tires rumbled over cobblestones. I kept my attention on the soft, purring sound to soothe my raw nerves.

Eventually, the pavement evened out, and the city disappeared behind us. We made our way along a darker road to reach the castle where the wedding reception would be held.

The historic edifice appeared as we rounded a curve, the stone façade shining under golden lights. Vicente had spared no expense on this sham of a wedding, inviting hundreds of people to witness his defiling of a young, unwilling girl. The ostentatious display was disgusting, but everyone in attendance seemed to think it was a joyous occasion.

The limo slowed to a stop, and Hugo ushered me out of the car. We stepped onto a red carpet, which led us through the open, massive wooden doors. More golden light spilled out into the night, welcoming us with false cheer. Marble floors shined under the massive crystal chandelier that lit the foyer.

Hugo wrapped his arm around my waist, but I stepped away as my stomach lurched. Over the years, I'd become numb to his touch. Tonight, it made my skin crawl. The memories of my own wedding night threatened to bubble up, and bile rose in my throat.

"Excuse me," I murmured. I couldn't come up with a good reason to leave Hugo's side, and I knew I'd pay for abandoning him later.

But all I could think about was fleeing from his slimy touch and rank scent.

I moved too quickly as I headed for the stairs, seeking privacy on the second level of the castle. No guests lingered around the banister on the upper floor, and I darted for the solace of a quiet room, where I could break down without witnesses.

The only thing worse than leaving Hugo standing alone in the foyer would be making a public scene. He'd be able to shrug off my sudden absence as the result of illness—I was sure I'd appeared pinched and pale enough in the limo to warrant that excuse.

No matter if the guests accepted his reasoning, he wouldn't allow me to go unpunished.

I could only hope that he'd wait until we were back on our estate. It was the most likely scenario. He wouldn't want to leave marks on me at this garish event; above all, he wanted others to believe that I truly was his devoted, loving wife. Anything less would be humiliating.

The second most powerful man in Bogotá couldn't have a disobedient wife. Hugo had made sure to break me and turn me into his adoring spouse a long time ago.

That had been after Adrián left me.

The boy I loved had left Colombia, and he'd never come

back. He let Hugo torment me and turn me into his perfectly polished, soulless plaything.

Now, Adrián lurked downstairs with the rest of the sharks. The man who'd glowered at me in the church might wear the boy's face, but he wasn't here to rescue me.

I'd given up on that foolish fantasy a long time ago, anyway.

I slipped into the first open room I found, closing the door behind me. Books lined the walls, gold lettering gleaming on darkly colored spines. The unique scent of leather-bound books helped calm me. The library on Hugo's estate was the place where I most often found solace from him, losing myself in fiction for hours. I took a deep breath, inhaling the familiar smell. It helped calm my nerves and my nausea.

The door clicked open behind me, and I spun with a shocked yelp.

"What the fuck do you think you're doing?" Hugo's ruddy cheeks were redder than usual, almost purple with rage.

I took a hasty step back, raising my hands to ward him off.

Surely, he wouldn't strike me. Not here. Not now.

I hadn't prepared myself for the pain of his fists yet.

He slammed the door shut behind him, advancing on me. I backed up farther, until my butt hit the desk behind me. He leaned over me, pressing his hips against mine to pin me in place.

"I'm sorry," I squeaked. "I'm not feeling well."

"I don't give a fuck how you're feeling." His spittle hit my cheek, and I cringed away. "You think you can embarrass me in front of all our guests?"

I shook my head wildly. "I didn't mean to. I'm sorry," I repeated, desperate.

He leaned closer, so I could feel his putrid breath on my

face. "I should bend you over this desk and fuck you raw." His cock jerked against my thigh as his cruel arousal rose along with his violence. "But I'd rather not have anyone hear you scream. You want to show me how sorry you are?"

I nodded frantically. "Yes. I really am sorry."

He stepped back. "Get on your knees. You know what to do."

The sick feeling in my gut intensified, my stomach churning. I sank to my knees, playing the part of obedient wife.

He quickly freed his cock from his slacks. It jutted toward my face, seeking the reluctant heat of my mouth.

I swallowed against the tang of bile on my tongue.

"Suck it," he seethed. "Show me you're sorry, and I won't beat the shit out of you when we get home."

Tears stung at the corners of my eyes as humiliation washed over me. I blinked them back. I wouldn't cry for him.

"Now," he snarled, thrusting his hips toward my lips.

I turned my face in revulsion, and his pre-cum wet my cheek.

He gripped my jaw, holding my head steady. "You'll pay for that later."

The door to the library opened, and my shame spiked. I couldn't bear to have anyone witness my degradation.

A fierce growl filled the room, and Hugo was ripped away from me. I watched in dumbstruck silence as Adrián tackled him to the floor. His massive fist connected with Hugo's jaw. My husband's head snapped to the side, blood spraying from his lips. Adrián didn't stop. He pummeled Hugo's face repeatedly, until crimson coated his knuckles and Hugo went completely still.

For a few long seconds, Adrián loomed over him, breathing hard. His lips peeled back from his teeth in a silent snarl, and his dark hair fell around his angular face, no longer arranged in its meticulous style.

Finally, he pushed to his feet and turned to me. He towered over me where I remained on my knees, frozen in place by shock at the sudden, violent display. His pale green eyes burned into me, and another feral sound slipped between his clenched teeth.

He reached for me with bloody hands. I shrank back, but that didn't deter him. His long fingers sank into my upper arms, yanking me to my feet.

He glowered at me for a moment, saying nothing. I shuddered in his grip, but I didn't dare struggle against him. I'd learned a long time ago that struggling only earned me more pain.

Hugo groaned, stirring at our feet.

Adrián's jaw ticked, but his shoulders relaxed, as though a decision had settled over him.

His grip shifted to my waist, and I shrieked as he tossed me over his shoulder.

His hand firmed on my upper thigh, squeezing hard enough to leave a mark. "Don't fight me," he ground out.

"What are you doing?" I asked, my voice shaking as fear suffused my system.

"I'm taking you."

One Click Stealing Beauty here!

THE BRATVA'S BABY

BY JANE HENRY

The wrought iron park bench I sit on is ice cold, but I hardly feel it. I'm too intent on waiting for the girl to arrive. The Americans think this weather is freezing, but I grew up in the bitter cold of northern Russia. The cold doesn't touch me. The ill-prepared people around me pull their coats tighter around their bodies and tighten their scarves around their necks. For a minute, I wonder if they're shielding themselves from me, and not the icy wind.

If they knew what I've done... what I'm capable of... what I'm planning to do... they'd do more than cover their necks with scarves.

I scowl into the wind. I hate cowardice.

But this girl... this girl I've been commissioned to take as mine. Despite outward appearances, she's no coward. And that intrigues me.

Sadie Ann Warren. Twenty-one years old. Fine brown hair, plain and mousy but fetching in the way it hangs in haphazard waves around her round face. Light brown eyes, pink cheeks, and full lips.

I wonder what she looks like when she cries. When she

smiles. I've never seen her smile.

She's five-foot-one and curvy, though you wouldn't know it from the way she dresses in thick, bulky, black and gray muted clothing. I know her dress size, her shoe size, her bra size, and I've already ordered the type of clothing she'll wear for me. I smile to myself, and a woman passing by catches the smile. It must look predatory, for her step quickens.

Sadie's nondescript appearance makes her easily meld into the masses as a nobody, which is perhaps exactly what she wants.

She has no friends. No relatives. And she has no idea that she's worth millions.

Her boss, the ancient and somewhat senile head librarian of the small-town library where she works won't even realize she hasn't shown up for work for several days. My men will make sure her boss is well distracted yet unharmed. Sadie's abduction, unlike the ones I've orchestrated in the past, will be an easy one. If trouble arises eventually, we'll fake her death.

It's almost as if it was meant to be. No one will know she's gone. No one will miss her. She's the perfect target.

I sip my bitter, steaming black coffee and watch as she makes her way up to the entrance of the library. It's eight-thirty a.m. precisely, as it is every other day she goes to work. She arrives half an hour early, prepares for the day, then opens the doors at nine. Sadie is predictable and routinized, and I like that. The trademark of a woman who responds well to structure and expectations. She'll easily conform to my standards... eventually.

To my left, a small cluster of girls giggles but quiets when they draw closer to me. They're college-aged, or so. I normally like women much younger than I am. They're more easily influenced, less jaded to the ways of men. These women, though, are barely women. Compared to Sadie's maturity, they're barely more than girls. I look away, but can feel their eyes taking me in, as if they think I'm stupid enough to not know they're staring. I'm wearing a tan work jacket, worn jeans, and boots, the ones I let stay scuffed and marked as if I'm a construction worker taking a break. With my large stature, I attract attention of the female variety wherever I go. It's better I look like a worker, an easy role to assume. No one would ever suspect what my real work entails.

The girls pass me and it grates on my nerves how they resume their giggling. Brats. Their fathers shouldn't let them out of the house dressed the way they are, especially with the likes of me and my brothers prowling the streets. It's freezing cold and yet they're dressed in thin skirts, their legs bare, open jackets revealing cleavage and tight little nipples showing straight through the thin fabric of their slutty tops. My palm itches to spank some sense into their little asses. I flex my hand.

It's been way, way too long since I've had a woman to punish.

Control.

Master.

These girls are too young and silly for a man like me.

Sadie is perfect.

My cock hardens with anticipation, and I shift on my seat.

I know everything about her. She pays her meager bills on time, and despite her paltry wage, contributes to the local food pantry with items bought with coupons she clips and sale items she purchases. Money will never be a concern for her again, but I like that she's fastidious. She reads books during every free moment of time she has, some non-fiction, but most historical romance books. That amuses me about her. She dresses like an amateur nun, but her heroines dress in swaths of silk and jewels. She carries a hard-covered book with her in the bag she holds by her side, and guards it with her life. During her break time, before bed, and when she first wakes up in the morning, she writes in it. I don't know yet what she writes, but I will. She does something with needles and yarn, knitting or something. I enjoy watching her weave fabric with the vibrant threads.

She fidgets when she's near a man, especially attractive, powerful men. Men like me.

I've never seen her pick up a cell phone or talk to a friend. She's a loner in every sense of the word.

I went over the plan again this morning with Dimitri.

Capture the girl.

Marry her.

Take her inheritance.

Get rid of her.

I swallow another sip of coffee and watch Sadie through the sliding glass doors of the library. Today she's wearing an ankle-length navy skirt that hits the tops of her shoes, and she's wrapped in a bulky gray cardigan the color of dirty dishwater. I imagine stripping the clothes off of her and revealing her creamy, bare, unblemished skin. My dick gets hard when I imagine marking her pretty pale skin. Teeth marks. Rope marks. Reddened skin and puckered flesh, christened with hot wax and my palm. I'll punish her for the sin of hiding a body like hers. She won't be allowed to with me.

She's so little. So virginal. An unsullied canvas.

"Enjoy your last taste of freedom, little girl," I whisper to myself before I finish my coffee. I push myself to my feet and cross the street.

It's time she met her future master.

One Click The Bratvas Baby here!

AWAKE

BY ASHLEIGH GIANNOCCARO

I hope you don't mind, but I let myself in, I had a key — well I found a key and used it. The door makes a squealing sound when it opens, don't worry, I'll oil the hinges for you tomorrow while you're at work. It won't take long, I promise. I'll be in and out, you won't even know I was here.

I talk to her inside my head, she left her laptop on, and her half finished glass of wine has a pink lipstick stain on the brim. Pink and orange sticky notes are stuck to every part of the table and around the screen of the computer. Touching the trackpad, I take a seat where she was sitting on the suede sofa, it's soft and silent. The screen flickers on and leaves her whole world open to me, photos, Facebook, Instagram even her bank statements are open. It's like every tab of her life is there tempting me, just one click away. The temptations, there are so many in here, but this will be the quietest so I start by opening her Facebook page and scrolling through her posts, pictures and friends. You can learn a lot from who a person blocks on social media, and she has only one on her list.

What did Maxwell C. Stone do to deserve that block? He looks like a good guy.

He's in some of her old photographs, holding hands, hugging, cheek kisses and other pathetic selfies. I'm glad to see her need to photograph her own face has died since then, selfies are such a vile habit. I pick up her glass and sip the wine she didn't finish, the rich Merlot slides smoothly down my throat. She has good taste in wine. The perfect pout of her lips is outlined on the glass, the pink of her lipstick remains there, leaving a piece of her behind. I lick it off, tasting her. It's waxy but sweet, and melts on my tongue with the next sip of wine. Moving on from Facebook, I look at all the other open tabs and documents on her computer. Her calendar pops up with a reminder, look how organized she is. Every detail of every day outlined down to the last five minutes. An alarm is set for eleven that says 'take your sleeping pill and go to bed' how efficient. I wonder why she needs that pill, her life seems so perfect. My attention skips from the screen to the Post-it notes she has tacked on to everything. Names, dates, numbers, and appointments already in the calendar. The green ones though -- they're different.

Don't call him.

He's not worth it.

You deserve better Ivy!

He smelled like sandalwood and leather

His hair was always perfect

His kisses were like cold water after a long run

He hurt you

Don't be stupid

These green ones are scattered between her other thoughts randomly, like she needs them to remind her of this heartache. I pluck them off, each one, stick them together and put them in my shirt pocket. She should really forget things like that, she doesn't need to think about him anymore. She will have plenty of other things to distract her. I smile and finish the last of the wine in her glass, putting it down where she had left it on a coaster that says 'keep calm' on it.

The small taste of wine has made me want more, I'm not done with my fact finding mission, so I go to her small kitchenette. The radio is playing softly, and I get the impression she's not fond of silence. Changing the station, I glance around at the spotlessly clean surfaces. The white and stainless steel appliances are all polished to a shine. In the corner, just like in the living room there is a small lamp that has been left on.

Are you afraid of the dark? Is that why you need a pill to go to sleep? Don't worry, I don't like the dark either. The music makes it so you won't hear things go bump in the night, most people these days leave the TV on, but you don't have one. Why not?

The open bottle of wine has been re-corked and stands on the counter beside the bowl of neatly arranged fruit. The one shiny red apple among the green ones calls to me, I take it and the wine back to the comfortable sofa. Shifting the throw pillows so that I'm comfortable, I put my feet up and bite the crunchy apple. I put down my wine and grab the small, black, leather-bound notebook from beside her computer. A number two pencil falls out onto my chest as I flip it open, every page is filled with doodles. Just black and white scribbles that cover every inch of every page. Cute cats, and monsters with knives, there's no theme at all. Food, flowers, and even faces fade into one another, making a never-ending animation of her life. It's like seeing inside her head while she dreams. I flip backwards from today's pictures to the front of the book where the gold embossed print says DREAM JOURNAL in block letters. She has scribbled a black cloud around the words and the rain falling from it is little frogs that are dying in animated 'pops' on the ground. The picture makes me smile, what must she see in her dreams? I am jealous of her. What I wouldn't give to close my eyes and dream, just for one night. To feel the weight of fatigue lifted and being able to fall down the sinkhole of unconsciousness, to turn off my mind just once, that would be bliss.

Sleep is a distant memory, something I have learned to live without, sometimes this insomnia induced madness makes me wonder if I shouldn't take a pill like she did. The fear of never waking up stops me.

I finish my apple while admiring Ivy's art, and seeing inside her thoughts. Placing the apple core and empty glass on the table, I look once more at her laptop, checking the files last saved.

Report.

That must be for her Eight-thirty am meeting. I delete it, and all traces of it from her computer with a smile that makes my cheeks ache. I get up and make sure to leave the sofa as it was, making sure my visit is only noticeable in the subtle clues. Just enough to make her think, not enough that she can't question her own sanity.

I wipe my hands on the guest towel in the small bathroom, before I take the three steps down the hall to stand in her open doorway. Her dressing gown is in a pile on the floor, I want to pick it up and fold it.

Not tonight. I'll let you sleep soundly tonight, maybe when I visit again I can clean up your room. You shouldn't leave that water bottle on your nightstand open, it could get knocked over and wet your phone. If you braid your hair it wouldn't get in your face like that, and everyone knows if you go to bed in a tank top you'll wake up with a boob hanging out. Maybe you should wear some proper pajamas, they do say you get better sleep in comfortable sleepwear. I worry those pills aren't good for you. Think about more natural remedies for that overactive mind of yours Ivy.

Again, I talk to her inside my head, she is fast asleep. The drugs make sure she doesn't sense me at all, they comatose her until morning. The little red clock illuminated next to her bed, she sets an alarm everyday. I'll let her be on time —today.

Read Awake for Free here!

MORE FREE BOOKS!

Beautifully Primal by Zoe Blake

Awake by Ashleigh Giannoccaro

Born to Be Bound by Addison Cain

Counsellor by Celia Aaron

41826842R00083

Printed in Poland
by Amazon Fulfillment
Poland Sp. z o.o., Wrocław